He looked quickly through the stack of letters. Employee unions, state environmental agencies, federal bureaus, fan mail. One letter was unopened. There was a lump in the middle of the brown envelope and on the outside his name had been printed with a warning: PERSONAL. CONFIDENTIAL.

The letter was handwritten on lined yellow paper. It was printed in block letters. It read:

MAYOR NOBILE. YOU ARE A BLOT UPON THE FACE OF AMERICA. THE ERASER RUBS OUT BLOTS. YOUR TIME IS COMING SOON.

It was signed: THE ERASER.

And taped to the bottom of the letter was half of a broken pencil, the eraser end.

Nobile scratched his head under the blue-black hair and, as was customary, looked at his fingertips as he withdrew his hand. Then he read the letter again.

On his private telephone line, he dialed a number he had never called before but had committed to memory. He did not know who was on the other end of the line.

When the dry voice answered, he said simply, “I’m in trouble.”

The Destroyer #38:
BAY CITY BLAST

Warren Murphy and Richard Sapir

DESTROYER BOOKS
WARREN MURPHY MEDIA LLC

This is a work of fiction. All the characters and events portrayed in this book are fictional, and any resemblance to real people or real incidents is purely coincidental.

THE DESTROYER #38: Bay City Blast

This edition published in 2021 by Destroyer Books/Warren Murphy Media LLC.

ISBN-13: 978-1-944073-64-0

ISBN-10: 1-944073-64-7

Requests for reproduction or interviews should be directed to DestroyerBooks@gmail.com.

Front cover art by Gere Tactical

For Karen
...and for the glorious House of Sinanju

CHAPTER ONE

IF JESUS HAD WALKED across the tiny cove that was the harbor of Bay City, New Jersey, no one would have bothered to think twice about it. The debris and rubble and flotsam and jetsam that packed the murky oily waters was so thick that *anyone* could have walked on the water there.

The city was tucked into two hundred acres of shoreline and upland on the coastline of New York Bay between Jersey City and Hoboken.

The upland was an average of only eighteen inches above sea level and when it rained for more than twelve minutes, every cellar in Bay City flooded. When Bay City was booming, no one had seemed to mind. There was plenty of money for plumbers. There was enough for everyone. Hot dog salesmen got rich. Loan sharks wore vicuna. The city's bookies wintered in Florida, at least until that time each year when they had to come back and remind their subordinates that honesty was the best policy.

The city had grown around its small seaport. Since the Thirties, graceful ocean-going liners and sturdy tankers had loaded and unloaded at the two concrete piers on either side of the bay twenty-four hours a day. The Holland Tunnel to New York City and New Jersey's heavy-duty road system were only minutes away. Bay City had blossomed. Twenty-two thousand people were packed into its small area, making it the most densely populated city in the United States.

It all came unglued right after the Korean War. New methods of shipping and larger ships required more upland area for trucks to park. They required deeper channels and bigger piers and the city fathers of Bay City refused to make any improvements in the harbor. One day everyone looked up and found that Bay City's shipping business had gone to Port Elizabeth to the south and to Hoboken to the north.

Like automobile rust, the process of urban deterioration was irreversible. By 1960, the population of Bay City had dropped to ten thousand. Fifteen years later, it had been cut in half again.

As people moved away in search of jobs elsewhere, the rats and rot that always threaten waterfront cities expanded unchecked.

Buildings quantum-leaped from full occupancy to abandoned ruin. Federal government grants allowed the city fathers to tear down most of the buildings, but there was no federal money to build new ones — and no people to move into them even if they had been built — and the skyline of Bay City wound up looking like a jack-o'-lantern's mouth, the wide-open spaces of vacant lots interrupted only by an occasional building.

Most of the five thousand persons left had jobs in the factories of Jersey City and Hoboken. The rest were pensioners too old or poor to move and kids and hustlers and degenerates and hookers and bums who preyed on each other and had no reason to move.

While Bay City's decline was inexorable, it was also gradual and therefore was not covered by the press, which dealt only in stories featuring explosions or non-negotiable demands. The city was just another declining eastern seaboard community, too small to rate any television exposure, either as contrast or color.

Few people visited the city, so it was noticed when one day a long black Cadillac limousine with California license plates pulled up in front of the Bay City Arms apartment house.

The Bay City Arms remained the only apartment building in town fit to inhabit. It was now 67 percent occupied and when the figure dropped below 60 percent, the out-of-town owner was going to dump the building back to the city for unpaid real estate taxes. The building's heat was turned off at 10:00 promptly each night and only one of the two elevators worked, but the building commanded an imposing view on its easterly side of the New York City skyline and the decayed concrete piers of Bay City.

As soon as the limousine pulled to the curb, two men jumped out of the back seat and closed the door behind them. One looked right and one looked left. The first man looked up, while the second looked behind them, scowling at the rooftops and windows of the nearby tenements. The first man went into the apartment lobby and looked around, then nodded out to the second man. Both men kept their right hands jammed deep into their jacket pockets.

The man on the sidewalk reopened the back door of the limousine and a short, sturdy man got out. He wore a highly fashionable black pinstripe suit. The man was in his early forties. His wavy hair was an unreal jet black and his skin was pockmarked but showed a healthy tan from a lot of time spent in the sun. The man smiled pleasantly as he stepped onto the sidewalk, but the man with his hand in his pocket did not smile and kept looking behind them as they walked toward the building lobby. Behind them, the chauffeur locked all the doors of the limousine, rolled his windows up, and kept the motor running.

The renting office in the back of the building was actually the superintendent's apartment. The superintendent was annoyed that he had to turn off "The Gong Show" to interview the prospective new tenant.

The interview was brief.

"My name is Rocco Nobile," said the well-tailored man with the blue-black hair. "I would like to rent the top floor."

"Very good, Mr. Nobile," said the superintendent. He was a short man with thinning hair and a surly scowl which had prompted tenants in the building to give him the nickname of "Happy." "We have a couple of very nice five-room apartments vacant there."

"You don't understand," said Nobile, smiling politely. "I want the top floor. The whole top floor."

"That's right," said one of the two men with hands in their pockets. "The whole top floor." He seemed about to say more but clamped his mouth tightly closed when Nobile glanced at him without a smile.

"But we can't...I'm sorry, Mr. Nobile. Two of the apartments on the top floor are already occupied."

"By whom?" asked Nobile. The two men with hands in their pockets nodded. They were proud to work for a man who said "whom."

"Mrs. Cochrane and the Gavins," Happy said.

"You have other apartments they can move into," Nobile said, and it was not a question.

Still Happy nodded.

Without turning in his chair, Rocco Nobile reached his hand up to his shoulder and snapped his fingers. One of the men left the room. Nobile asked Happy for a cup of coffee, black, without sugar, while they waited.

Before he had finished the coffee, the man returned to the apartment "They'll move by the weekend," he said.

"Errrr, what'd you say to them?" asked Happy.

Before the man could answer, Nobile spoke. "Mr. Happy," he said, "my man was very nice to them. I am not wishing to cause trouble but I need the entire top floor. I entertain a great deal and I conduct my business from my home. I empowered my man to make them a very handsome cash offer if they would switch apartments. Apparently they have accepted. I am glad. I want only to be a good neighbor."

Happy looked at the man who had just returned to the apartment.

"That's right," the man said. "Empowered. Me." He nodded.

Rocco Nobile's good neighbors on the fourteenth floor moved to lower floors the next day, with moving men paid by Rocco Nobile helping them, and with checks for two thousand dollars each in their pockets. That same day, an ant horde of carpenters and contractors and plasterers swarmed into the top floor, knocking out walls and joining the four apartments into one enormous penthouse suite. They were finished in one day.

The decorators arrived the next morning. The furniture they selected arrived that afternoon.

Rocco Nobile moved in Saturday morning.

On Saturday afternoon, his two companions rented a vacant store a block from the city's piers and two blocks from the old yellow brick City Hall. A hastily hired sign painter erected a large sign over the windows.

The Bay City Improvement Association
Rocco Nobile, Standard Bearer

Two young women were hired to staff the office. They were told they were to act as a clearing house for city residents seeking information on federal aid programs, about welfare, about Social Security benefits, about recreational programs available. The existence of the new office was announced the following Wednesday with an advertisement in the small twice-weekly paper which was Bay City's only media link with civilization.

Two days later, the Bay City Improvement Association announced that it was making plans to open a privately funded day care center to watch over the children of working parents. A day later, Rocco Nobile, standard bearer of the Bay City Improvement Association, announced that he had received a contribution from an anonymous donor which would enable the association to set up a free medical clinic for Bay City residents who could not afford private doctors.

After a week of such announcements, it should have begun to get through to the drink-sodden editor of the *Bay City Bugle* that something unusual was happening in Bay City, but it hadn't.

As he was sitting in his regular tavern for his morning eye-opener, the drinker on the next stool said to him: "Hey, that Rocco Nobile is something, hah?"

"Who's Rocco Nobile?" the editor asked as he waved to the bartender for another stinger on the rocks.

"That guy you keep writing about in the paper who's doing all those good things."

"Oh, sure," said the editor. He smiled. Maybe his friend would buy the drink if he said he liked Rocco Nobile. "A great man," the editor said. "I'm going to do a big feature story on him."

"Hey, that's good," said the man on the next stool. "Let me buy you that drink."

The editor did not notice that all the while the man talked to him, he kept his right hand jammed into his jacket pocket.

The next day the editor remembered Rocco Nobile and telephoned for an appointment. He was ushered into Nobile's office and sitting room that very afternoon, and he spoke with Nobile for two hours and it might have been longer except he refused, absolutely refused, to have Mr. Nobile go to the trouble of sending out for another bottle of Creme de Menthe to make more stingers on the rocks.

The next day, the *Bay City Bugle* announced that Rocco Nobile, a self-made multi-millionaire who had made a giant fortune in the oil importing business, had moved to Bay City.

His goal, he said, was to "do what little I can" to revitalize the city and to get the piers working again.

Rocco Nobile said that he owed Bay City a debt he wanted to repay because when his great-grandparents had come to America seventy-five years earlier, they had settled first in Bay City. "I want to repay our family's debt to this great land of freedom and opportunity," Nobile said. In parentheses, the editor added: "A fine and noble sentiment. Would that more of us felt that way."

Before the story appeared, Nobile told his secretary in her office, "When that drunk's story appears, you're going to hear from the mayor. He'll want to talk to me. Tell him that I'm going to be in and out of town for the next few days. Make the appointment for next Wednesday. Here."

Mayor Douglass Windlow called on time as Nobile had expected and the appointment was made for the following week.

In the meantime, Nobile's men prowled the city day and night, buying drinks in taverns, courtesy of Rocco Nobile. They visited homes, dispensing leaflets on aid programs for the elderly and sick, courtesy of Rocco Nobile. They talked a lot, but they listened more.

Mayor Douglass Windlow arrived at 2 P.M. on Wednesday. Nobile asked if he would join him in a small glass of Amaretto, then sat in an upholstered chair across from the mayor, who sat casually on the leather sofa.

"What is on your mind, Mayor?"

Windlow showed Nobile the blinding smile which was his greatest political asset, sipped the Amaretto and said, "I just thought I should meet you. For a new man in town, you've made a considerable impact already."

"Thank you. I hope to do more."

The mayor put down his glass and fidgeted with one of his gold cufflinks for a moment.

"Rebuilding a city like this is a terribly hard job," he said. "Everything that the urban crisis is going to be all over the nation is already here. Dwindling resources, a shrinking tax base, an impoverished population requiring more and more services with fewer and fewer tax dollars to pay for them. This city is a whole catalog of urban ills." The mayor slid into the phrases easily and smoothly, as befitting one who had learned them through years of giving exactly the same speech.

"Well," Nobile said with a slight smile. "It's not that bad for some."

Mayor Windlow looked at him, a puzzled expression on his face.

"Your brother-in-law, for instance," said Nobile, still smiling.

"My brother-in-law?"

"Yes," Nobile said. "The one who is the secret owner of the paving company which does all the city's work." He took a notebook from the side pocket of his smoking jacket and carefully opened it to a page. "Yes. Your wife's brother, Fred."

He looked up at Mayor Windlow and this time Nobile wasn't smiling. Windlow gulped. He started to answer, opened his mouth, then closed it again.

"And of course there are other people in town who make a very good living. For instance, there is Peppy Ritale, who handles the numbers play in town. He does quite well. Naturally, he would do much better if he did not have to pay you twenty-five percent of his profits each week," Nobile said. "And there is Mr. Bangston, who is the loanshark down on River Street. Another partner of yours. And there is..." He stopped and snapped the book closed. The crack of the hard cover lingered in the room like the sound of a pistol shot. "But I guess there isn't any need in going on. You know the names in this book."

Windlow picked up his glass of Amaretto and drained it in one large swallow.

"Who are you?" he finally said. "What do you want?"

"I am who I say. Rocco Nobile. And I am going to be the next mayor of Bay City."

"The election's two years off," Windlow said.

"I am not waiting for the election," Nobile said. "I will be appointed, after you resign, to fill your unexpired term."

Windlow tried a small smile. "Oh, you have it all worked out," he said. "I resign, you take over. But suppose I just don't resign?"

Nobile shrugged. "Then I will have to wait until the federal prosecutors indict you for all the crimes in this book. That will put me several months off schedule, but I guess I could wait if I had to."

There was a long, uneasy pause in the room.

"You can prove those things?" the mayor said, pointing toward the notebook which lay on the table between them. His hand quivered as if he were toying with the idea of grabbing the notebook and fleeing.

"You know I can," Nobile said. "I would be a poor fool to aim a gun at you, without being sure first that it was loaded."

"There's room enough in Bay City for everybody. I could use a partner," Windlow said hopefully. "I've been thinking for a long time now that some new blood might...well, might improve things here. A fresh outlook. There *is* enough for everybody."

"Wrong," Nobile said. "There is barely enough for me. But there will be." His dark eyes narrowed as he stared at Mayor Douglass Windlow. He said casually, "I think next week would be a good time for you to resign."

"The City Commission would have to elect my successor," Windlow said. "I can't just appoint you."

Nobile picked up the notebook again and opened it to a section near the back.

"Yes, here it is. The City Commission. I have a numbers runner, a man who sells police cars to the city in violation of the law and a man who gets kickbacks from all municipal employees for tickets to testimonial dinners that are never held. That is three out of five. I will have no trouble getting their votes."

"No, I guess you won't," Windlow said. He sank back in the soft sofa. "Got any more Amaretto?"

"No," said Nobile. "I see no point in lengthening this meeting unnecessarily since I find it uncomfortable. You resign next Friday. By the following Monday, I want you to be moving to your house at the New Jersey shore." Nobile smiled. "You know. The house which is secretly owned in your wife's maiden name."

Windlow sighed heavily and nodded.

He stood up. "You don't mind, I suppose, if I don't shake your hand," he said bitterly.

"Not while I wear expensive rings on my fingers," Nobile said. "Good day, Mayor."

As Windlow reached the door, Nobile called to him.

"Mayor, I think that no one should know about this until you submit your resignation at next Friday's meeting of the City Commission. And of course you will simply cite health reasons for your decision."

"Of course. What about that notebook?"

"I will hold onto it," Nobile said, "against the day when you might foolishly think of attempting a political comeback."

He walked to his bar and poured himself another glass of Amaretto. "But of course you won't do that, Mayor. Will you?"

The mayor nodded and walked from the room.

Rocco Nobile sipped his Amaretto casually while looking out the large glass windows toward the small unused port of Bay City. He finished the glass and set it down on the windowsill and went to a telephone on the desk in the corner of the room.

He dialed a New York number and waited until the telephone was answered.

Nobile said simply, "It's ours." He paused, listening. "That's right. The whole city. We own it."

CHAPTER TWO

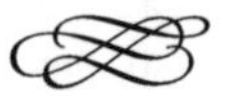

HIS NAME WAS REMO and and he owned nothing.

He had no automobile. When he needed one, he rented it, and when he was done with it, he just left it at the side of the road, because it gave him pleasure to imagine the face of his superior when the bill came in.

He bought clothes when he needed them, using a variety of credit cards in a variety of names, and when the clothes were dirty, he generally just threw them away.

He owned no house. He had spent the last ten years in hotel rooms, and he had no name, no family, no friends, no past and no future.

Definitely no future.

He told himself that as he sat in the fork of an oak tree, twenty-five feet above the ground, looking through the big picture windows of a secluded lakeside home waiting for all the guests of honor to show up.

Fifteen had arrived, but there were still two more due. Remo would wait. He wanted them all. He thought about that for a moment, and then realized he did own something after all. He owned his self-respect and that came from pride in doing his job well.

But no friends. Another car came up the driveway of the home and parked at the side of the long row of Cadillacs and Mercedes. Two men got out and walked toward the house. Remo recognized one as the man he had been expecting. The second man was obviously his lawyer because he had a gold pen and pencil set in his outside jacket pocket and only lawyers carried pens and pencils there.

One more guest to go.

No friends. The closest thing to a friend Remo had was Chiun, the eighty-year-old Korean who was the latest Master of Sinanju, an age-old house of assassins. But he wasn't a friend. He was Remo's trainer and a confidant and like the father that Remo had never had. But not a friend.

There was Dr. Harold W. Smith, head of the secret organization CURE that had trained Remo to kill America's enemies. But Smith was no man's friend. Who could love Smith? Maybe Mrs. Smith. Maybe his accountant, who was taken by the CURE director's passion for neatness. Nobody else.

There was Ruby Gonzalez, the one-time CIA agent who now worked as Smith's head assistant in CURE — the only person besides Remo and Smith and the President of the United States who knew what CURE was. And even Ruby wasn't a friend. Remo respected her brains and her toughness, but the young black woman came from a world different from Remo's, and your friends were usually those who had shared the springs and summers of your life.

That was it. Everybody else Remo knew or met were people he had been ordered to kill.

Another car arrived, kicking up gravel on the roadway beneath Remo's feet as he sat in the tree. It was a Continental Mark Four, which the owner had seemed determined, by sheer tastelessness, to promote to a Mark Ten. The auto was littered with chrome and rabbit tails and pinstripes and special hood medallions. The driver was alone. He had a red face and sandy hair and Remo recognized him as the last guest, Lee-Bob Barkins, who had killed his wife with a chainsaw and then tried to use her body for chum while shark fishing off the Alabama coast. Unfortunately, while he had been using her left hand for bait, a passing boat had snagged his line and ripped off the hook and hand. Lee-Bob Barkins had fled, but the other boat had gotten his boat's ID number and police were able to identify the dead woman from some identifying scars on her left hand, suffered three years earlier when Lee-Bob, a good old boy in a bet with some other good old boys, had taken to her with a hunting knife.

Lee-Bob at his trial had claimed he was framed, but he had been convicted of murder, sentenced to life, but then was pardoned after serving fourteen months, as an outgoing governor turned the jails loose.

He had released rapists and murderers and arsonists and kidnappers and terrorists. All had one thing in common. They had money.

Seventeen of the worst were now inside, in the lakefront home of Sam Speer, the outgoing governor's closest adviser, friend and confidant, for which, Remo knew, in politics you read bagman.

Seventeen men and Speer. That was tonight's assignment. There were also ten assorted lawyers who might get in the way, but that didn't bother Remo. There were too many lawyers anyway. Nobody ever got criticized for killing a lawyer.

Remo pushed himself out of the fork of the tree and dropped the twenty-five feet to the ground. He landed without a sound, his feet moving in a walking motion even before he touched ground.

He looked in the picture window in time to see the men raising champagne glasses in a toast.

Fragments of conversation drifted out to Remo's ears.

"...act of mercy and charity."

"...in case of an investigation, don't say anything."

"...charity, my ass...cost me two hundred thousand."

"...cost us all two hundred thousand."

"...let anybody hear that and you'll be back in."

Remo recognized Sam Speer, the outgoing governor's right-hand man. He was a big, fattish man with a simian swoop of dark hair growing low across his forehead and hooded eyes that made him look as if he were just ready to doze off.

He was the governor's friend, Remo thought. Even that governor had a friend. And these seventeen animals in the Sam Speer living room. They probably had friends too. Somebody at least thought enough of them to put up two hundred thousand dollars each to get them out of jail. Maybe they had families as well as friends.

And Remo had neither.

He didn't think it was fair. Some guys had all the luck.

He thought about that while he walked around the back of the house and down to the lake, where he idly tossed stones into the water. Remo wore black trousers and a black T-shirt and he knew that, from the house, he would be lost in the shadows and invisible. He was a thin man with dark hair and eyes as deep as night and the only sign that he might have been something unusual were his thick wrists, which he frequently flexed and rotated as if they caused him discomfort.

Family and friends.

He had been recruited into CURE just because he had no family. He was an orphan, a cop on the Newark police force, and then one night he was framed for a murder he didn't commit, sent to an electric chair which didn't work, and when he woke up, he had been told he was working for CURE, a secret agency set up to fight crime. If he didn't want to work for CURE, they would just have finished the job the electric chair was supposed to have done.

He had been warned at the start. "You'll have no friends, Remo Williams. You'll have no family. You'll have no place you can call home. All you'll have is a sense that maybe, just maybe, you can do something to make America better."

He had thought it was bullshit then, and now, more than a decade later, he still thought it was bullshit. But he did not leave, and he knew why he stayed. Because CURE and the training of Sinanju had given Remo the only thing he had ever had in his life. Self-respect. Pride in his work. And nobody could take that away from him.

Behind him, from the front door of the house, Remo heard sounds and he drifted back through the darkness under the trees.

Two men were leaving the home of Sam Speer. One he recognized as Billy-Ben Bingham, a particularly vicious rapist who had been released after serving ten years of a life sentence. The man with him looked lawyerly. They headed for a car and Remo moved up next to the car in the darkness. When the motors had started and the lawyer backed the car up and made a turn in the driveway to head back toward the road, Remo opened the front door and slid in next to the rapist.

"Who...?" said the driver.

"What the...?" said the rapist.

"Hi," said Remo. "Just drive. I'm getting out soon."

The rapist's hands were at his throat but they closed on air and Remo put him away with an economical right index finger into the right kidney area. The rapist *whooshed* and slumped forward against the dashboard's digital clock between Remo and the lawyer, who threw the car into parking gear and reached for the door handle.

Remo's left hand pulled him back inside the car. Remo's right hand dropped the gear shift into "drive" and steered the car down the driveway, out onto the road, and made a right-hand turn.

Twenty-five yards down the road was a sign posted by the lakeside homeowners association, explaining that it wanted to keep out bad elements. On the right side was a small roadway leading down to a boat ramp. The way the lawyer's head flopped at the end of Remo's left hand, he knew the man's neck had snapped. Remo drove to the water's edge, dropped the gear shift in "low," and stomped on the gas pedal. As the car surged, he slipped out the door and watched as the car hurried down the slight incline, hit the edge of a wooden dock, teetered momentarily, then dropped into the waters of the lake.

The car hit with a *splat* and a *sizzle.* It began to sink but Remo did not stay to watch it because he was already moving back toward the house. He had to be careful that a big bunch of them didn't all leave at once, because then he would have to dispose of them on the lawn and that could get messy.

He waited in the tree again and heard Sam Speer's voice telling them that it would be safest if they continued to leave one at a time. "Just in case."

Remo nodded with satisfaction. "Good for you," he mumbled to himself. "Good for you."

The next one was Lee-Bob Barkins, who got into his Lincoln, recklessly swerved it around and started up the driveway. As he passed under Remo's tree, Remo let himself drop down onto the roof of the car. The driver's window was open and Remo turned his body sideways on the roof of the car, and reached his left hand through the open window and put it around Lee-Bob's throat.

"Hi, fella," Remo said.

Lee-Bob saw the head hanging upside down in the driver's window and he wanted to reach out and crush it, but the pressure around his own throat was too great.

"Twenty five yards down the road, hang a right," Remo said.

Lee-Bob hit the brakes and the car stopped.

"C'mon," Remo said. "I don't have all night."

He slipped off the car's roof, still holding onto Lee-Bob's throat, pushed the man roughly across the seat and got in behind the wheel.

"Who are you?" Lee-Bob managed to sputter.

"I'm the welcome wagon," Remo said. "Come to make your brief stay in the outside world as pleasant as possible. Goodbye."

He heard the bones separate in the neck as he turned into the small roadway leading to the boat ramp. Behind him, he heard voices in the doorway of the Speer house.

"Damn," Remo said. "Hurry, hurry, hurry."

He got out of the car, aimed its wheels straight down toward the water, then wedged Lee-Bob Barkins under the dashboard against the gas pedal. He closed the door behind him, dropped the gear shift into "drive," and the car gunned down the slight hill. Remo did not wait to hear the splash. Two more men were getting into a car in front of Speer's house.

He caught that car on the road. In it was Jimmy-Joe Jepson, an arsonist whose fires had killed twenty-three persons. Remo decided that putting everybody into the lake was too time-consuming, so he just turned off the key after killing Jimmy-Joe and his lawyer, and let the car roll down the road until it stopped, nose-first, against a tree.

It was getting complicated now. Remo reached into the pocket of his black T-shirt and took out a list. Right. He had Lee-Bob Barkins. And he had Billy-Ben Bingham. And he had Jimmy-Joe Jepson. Plus assorted attorneys. But they weren't on the list. Tonight lawyers were a bonus he would give Smith for free, just as a part of his annual contribution to the good of the republic.

By the time he reached the seventeenth car, the roadway leading from Speer's house was pretty full, so Remo took Tim-Tom Tucker and his lawyer in the driveway, before they even started their car.

Remo looked at his list again. Every one of them. He had them all. He snapped his index finger against the list with satisfaction. "There," he said. "Now nobody can complain about that."

He walked to the front door of the house, unlocked because even though the crime rate in the South was the highest in the nation, it wasn't crime that took place in houses. It was generally just senseless violence that Remo thought came out of a streak of viciousness that ran deep through the Southern character. It exploded in saloons and parking lots and on street corners, but it was rarely premeditated so no one ever had to lock their doors. Remo was glad he did not have to live in the South. Angry violence annoyed him as a waste of energy.

He strolled inside the house and found Sam Speer in the living room, pouring the last of a bottle of champagne into an oversized brandy snifter.

"Who are you?" Speer asked as he turned to face Remo.

"My name is Remo."

"What do you want?"

"What I want is some time off to go fishing," Remo said. "But what I got is to kill you."

"Not a chance, Buddy," Speer said. He reached inside his jacket, very quickly for such a big man, and pulled a .38 caliber revolver from a shoulder holster.

Remo shook his head.

He frowned. "Don't waste my time with that," he said.

Speer raised the gun at Remo and squeezed the trigger.

He blinked his eyes at the sound of the report. When he opened them, Remo was not standing in front of him. Nor was he on the floor in a bloodied heap.

"You're not a nice person," he heard Remo say. "Just because you're a fat, ugly schemer who would steal a hot stove and come back for the smoke doesn't mean you couldn't try to be a nice person."

Speer felt the tap on his left shoulder, but before he could spin around and fire again, he felt a sharp burst of pain in the center of his back. Normally, the brain could tell a body what kind of pain it was suffering from and where, but the brain relied on impulses that traveled along the spinal cord, and here Speer's spine had been snapped, so he felt nothing and knew nothing after the first burst of pain and instead just slowly slumped to the oak flooring of the house.

On a table, Remo saw a large pile of money. It should have been seventeen payments of two hundred thousand dollars each. He calculated quickly and decided that that would be more than a million dollars. Maybe even two million.

And because he had just heard on the news that inflation was caused by excess money in circulation, he started a fire in the fireplace and burned the money before he left.

Remo had left his car in the parking lot of the Ding-Dong Diner, only three miles away, so he walked because it was a nice night. The birds sang in the trees under the bright Southern moon and there was just enough breeze to cool the air, and it was the kind of night that made a man glad to be alive, Remo thought.

Chiun was still sitting in the passenger's seat of the rented automobile, watching the front door of the diner which had been converted from an old railroad car.

The frail old man did not turn around as Remo opened the unlocked door and slid behind the wheel. Instead, his hands folded inside the billowing sleeves of his dark green evening kimono, he watched the front door of the diner with intense concentration.

"All done," Remo said.

"Shhhh," said Chiun. "This is very interesting."

"What's very interesting?"

"This is a place to eat, correct?" Chiun asked.

"That's right."

"Everybody who goes inside is already fat," Chiun said. "If they are already fat, why are they going in there to eat?"

"Even fat people have to eat," Remo said.

Chiun turned his hazel eyes on Remo and stared at him with disdain.

"Who told you that?" he asked.

"Listen. I do a big night's work and all you're interested in is fat people eating?" Remo started the car and drove over the pitted ruts of the diner driveway, out onto Route 123, heading north.

Chiun sighed. "I suppose now I must listen to your boring account of how you spent your evening," he said.

"No, you don't. It's not important. Twenty-seven guys, that's all. Twenty-eight if you count the one who wasn't a nice person."

"Paaaah. And faaaaah. It is a nothing," Chiun said. "Numbers are not important. What is important is attitude and performance. Was your elbow straight? Did you take pride in doing adequate work? These things are important."

"Strangely enough, Little Father, I did," Remo said as he turned off Route 123 and headed east toward the coast on County Road 456, a narrow, unlighted two-lane road. "I thought to myself that all I have in this world is self-respect for a job well done."

"Adequately done, knowing you," Chiun said.

"Well done," Remo insisted. They were silent for a few moments. Remo said, "Funny, to think of being proud about killing."

"Killing?" said Chiun. His voice scaled the heights of outrage. "Killing? You call the work of an assassin mere killing? Booms kill."

"Bombs," Remo corrected.

"Yes," said Chiun. "And they are not proud. Bullets kill. They are not proud either. Are germs proud? Yet who kills more than germs? I remember once, a particular bad sort of germ which carried off almost half my native village of Sinanju."

"Halfway measures are never any good," Remo said. Chiun ignored him.

"But those germs were not proud. Now, you are not a boom."

"Bomb."

"Or a bullet or a germ. You are an assassin. If you do well or, in your case, adequately, you must be proud. Really, Remo." Chiun's hands had come from his sleeves and fluttered in front of his face as he spoke. "Really, you surprise me. If you were a doctor or a lawyer or some other menial, I could understand not being proud. But an assassin? Trained by Sinanju? Not being proud? It staggers me."

"No," Remo said, "you're wrong. I am proud. I'm proud of your teaching me Sinanju and me learning it. I'm proud of being an assassin. I'm proud of keeping my elbows straight when I work. I'm proud of kill...ooops, assassinating twenty-eight men tonight."

"Good," said Chiun, warmly. "Perhaps you will yet learn what is important in life."

"And I'm proud to be an American, fellas," Remo said. "Really proud. When those 'Stars and Stripes Forever' come marching by on the Fourth of July, I get this warm feeling that I'm ten feet tall and put on earth by God to help the little folks of the rest of the world solve their problems, the good old-fashioned American way. Yessirreebob, proud to be an American."

Chiun sniffed. "There are some types of river mud which one not only cannot make into diamonds, but cannot even make into bricks. Woe is me. It was my misfortune to find one such as you."

Their motel room was on a spit of land that jutted out into the Atlantic Ocean and when they returned to it, Chiun immediately went to his thirteen lacquered steamer trunks that went with him wherever he went and began to check the contents. Chiun said, depending on his mood, that the trunks contained his few meager possessions, or that they contained his most valuable treasures without which he could not live. Remo, however, had seen inside the trunks and knew that they contained primarily a year-long supply of satin and silk kimonos, Cinzano ashtrays, hotel towels, free matchbooks, coaster and cocktail stirrers, complimentary Frisbees, plastic shoe-shine cloths, key chains and everything else that Chiun could pick up free or on the cheap. One trunk was filled, top to bottom, with Gideon Bibles that Chiun had stolen from the hotel rooms they had stayed in over the last ten years.

"Why do you keep checking those things?" Remo asked. He addressed the question to Chiun's back as the old Oriental was bent over a trunk, examining its contents.

Without turning, Chiun raised a finger as if making a high point in his lecture on life.

"Chambermaids. They steal things."

"But cheap Cinzano ashtrays? Who'd steal those?"

"There are more things in my trunks than ashtrays," Chiun said and his voice was chilled. "Many valuable things."

"I know," Remo said. "But I don't think the chambermaid would risk getting killed so she could rip off your complimentary dinner napkin from Disney World."

"You know nothing," Chiun said. He continued his inspection. The telephone rang, and Remo knew it was Dr. Harold W. Smith, checking on the evening's work.

"Done," he said. "Yeah. All of them."

"Good," Smith said.

"Yes, I was," Remo said. "Very good tonight."

"Tell him you are proud to be an American," Chiun suggested.

"I'm proud to be an American, assassinating people for you," Remo told Smith.

"Yes, yes. Well, there is something I want you to do," Smith said.

"Dammit, Smitty, how about some time off?"

"This is time off," Smith said.

"I'm not going to kill anybody," Remo said. "No matter how proud I am."

"Good," said Smith. "That's just what I want. I don't want you to kill anybody. I just want you to look around."

"Look around at what? Where?"

"Bay City, New Jersey. Something's going on up there and we want to get a little handle on it. I'd like you to go up there and just try to get the feel of the town. Tell me what you think."

"You don't have anybody else you can send in there? This isn't my kind of work," Remo said.

"Nothing is," Chiun said.

"I know," Smith said. "But as a favor to me."

"Say that again?" Remo asked.

"Do this as a favor to me."

"Since you put it that way," Remo said. "Bay City, here we come."

CHAPTER THREE

THE FIRST THING REMO and Chiun noticed in Bay City was a large policeman whose body attacked his blue uniform from inside, like sausage filling threatening its casing as it neared the boiling point in a pot of water. The policeman was swinging his night stick, walking toward a corner newsstand only two blocks from the city's piers.

An old woman was buying a newspaper at the stand. After she had the newspaper in her hand, she handed the newsstand man a coin, wrapped up in a piece of paper. He nodded, and she smiled and walked away.

When the woman left, the policeman went to the newsstand and the operator reached in under the shelf where he kept his money. Remo saw him take something out. He took a newspaper and pulled it down below the level of the shelf on which the papers sat. A moment later, he handed the newspaper out to the policeman, who tucked it tightly under his left arm, touched the bill of his cap with his nightstick and strolled off down the street.

Remo watched him through the windows of a car parked across the street. Halfway down the block, the policeman ducked into a hallway. His back was to Remo but Remo could see he was fiddling with the newspaper. As the policeman turned back, Remo saw him tuck something into the inside pocket of his uniform blouse. It made a small lump inside the jacket. The cop strolled down the steps, still holding the newspaper in his left hand. Ten feet down the block, he dropped the paper into a litter basket.

"So," Remo said aloud. "The cops are protecting gambling."

"You can tell this by watching a policeman buy a newspaper?" Chiun said.

"I've seen it before. The guy at the newsstand is booking numbers. The cop comes by and the bookie gives him an envelope with the protection money."

"If he needs protection, why does he not hire us?" Chiun asked.

"He can't afford us. And it's not that kind of protection. It's just protection against getting arrested. Now the cop takes the money back to his headquarters or wherever and gives it to his captain or his chief, and the cops get a small piece for looking the other way and not arresting anybody."

"And the rest of the money?"

"The top cop gets some and the rest of it goes to whatever politician has made the deal with the bookies."

"The economy of this country is very complex," Chiun said. "How is it that you understand it, when you do not understand many things well at all?"

"When I was a cop, I saw it all the time in Newark. That's not far from here."

"And did you do this?" Chiun asked. "Did you take this money to protect these numerals?"

"Numbers," Remo said. "No. I was a straight cop. But I saw it done a lot. Usually cops aren't so brazen about it. Let's follow him."

They made a U-turn in the middle of the street and drove slowly down the block after the policeman, parking frequently to wait and watch.

They saw the policeman visit two more news stands. He picked up two more folded newspapers, dipped into two more hallways to remove their contents, then threw the newspapers away in trash baskets.

The trash baskets were bright orange with large black letters that read:

Bay City Improvement Association

Mayor Rocco Nobile, Standard Bearer

While he was stopped at the curb, Remo saw a long black limousine pass them. The back windows were shrouded behind Venetian blinds.

"Not the kind of car you'd expect to find in this town," he said.

"It is the third such automobile that has passed us in the last hour," Chiun said.

"You sure?"

"Yes."

"Not the same car?"

"Not unless they keep changing those identification numbers on the front of it, just to confuse us."

"That's interesting," Remo said.

"If you say so," said Chiun.

As they drove from the curb and turned the corner, they saw the burly policeman walk into the storefront offices of the Bay City Improvement Association.

"That's interesting," Remo said.

"You find everything interesting today," Chiun said. "You are not going to try to become a detective again, are you?"

"No," said Remo. "I'm just doing what Smitty wants. Keeping an eye on the place. But I could've been a detective. I could've been a good one. I just didn't have any political connections so I could never get promoted to detective."

"Probably wise for the city of Newark," Chiun said.

"Oh, yeah?"

"Pfaaah," said Chiun.

"There's nothing wrong with being a detective," said Remo. "For instance, there's something funny going on here. That cop should've gone back to his precinct to turn in that money. If he's dropping it off here at a political headquarters, that means one of two things."

"And of course you will tell me what they are?"

"Yes, I will," Remo said. "One, it means that politicians, probably this Rocco Nobile, has got his hand in the numbers on an operational level, which is brazen. Two, it means that he's pretty sure he's safe because he hasn't busted the chain between the cop pickup man and himself. That's brazen too. He must figure he's got a tight lock on this town."

"Maybe he just wants everybody to know how powerful he is," Chiun said.

"That's ridiculous," Remo said. "Why would he want to do that?"

"I don't know. You're the detective," said Chiun. He had his fingers together in steeple fashion and was tapping the tips together in rhythmic patterns, first thumb to thumb, then index to index, and down to the little fingers; then offsetting the rhythms by ones, first thumb to index, and index to middle, and middle to ring, and ring to small finger, and small finger to thumb; and then skipping by twos, thumb to middle, index to small. It was a dexterity exercise he did only when he was bored.

Five minutes later, the burly policeman came out of the Bay City Improvement Association headquarters. Remo could tell from the flatness on the left front part of his uniform that he had dropped off his envelopes of money. The policeman walked casually down the street toward the riverfront. The street was a garish blend of neighborhood bars and disco joints and even in the morning, bright neon lights flickered on and off along the thoroughfare.

Another black limousine passed them and Remo decided to follow it. The Cadillac went down two blocks to River Street, the thoroughfare which ran the width of the city from pier to pier. It turned right and stopped, and Remo parked at the corner. The limo had stopped in front of an old loft building whose peeling paint faintly showed the old legend: Christine's Shirt Factory.

Two green-and-white moving vans were in front of the building and using heavy pulleys, the workers were lifting heavy printing equipment and photostatic copiers up to a second-floor loft. Inside the building, Remo could hear the sounds of carpentry, hammering and electric saws.

The limousine disgorged from its back seat a medicine ball of a man in a pinstripe suit who nodded approvingly at the equipment moving in. He waved at the workmen to speed things up. As his hands moved through the morning sunlight, diamond rings glistened on his fingers. He looked like a dew-covered mushroom, shining at daybreak.

Remo nodded to himself and drove away. Two blocks farther down

River Street, the scene was being repeated in front of another loft building. Movers, equipment, workmen refurbishing the building, another black limousine and another Mafia-type with pinky rings and pinstripe suit watching approvingly.

Four blocks farther north, the scene was repeated again.

"A lot of moving in for a town that's supposed to be on the skids," Remo said.

Chiun stopped doing his finger exercises. He looked at Remo, then glanced out the window at the litter that filled the streets. "Perhaps the world has suddenly discovered the charms of this beautiful American city."

Remo grunted and turned the rented car away from the waterfront, back toward their motel in Jersey City. He dropped Chiun off at their rooms, then drove back to the honky-tonk block in Bay City where the Rocco Nobile Improvement Association was headquartered.

Remo parked and walked casually up the street, turning into the doorway of the Roaring Twenties Lounge. One portion of its front window was unpainted, in the form of a heart. Inside the cutout were fly-specked pictures of female impersonators who appeared in the club's show every Saturday night. The pictures were yellowed with age and the corners were pulling away from the red velvet back on which they had been taped.

Inside, Remo stepped to the dark bar and ordered a Scotch on the rocks with a glass of water side.

He paid a dollar fifty from a five-dollar bill and when he got his change, tried to sip the water. The water in Bay City came from the Jersey City water system, pumped through century-old pipes that leaked out water and sucked up dirt. The water tasted as if it had been filtered through used kitty litter.

Remo smelled it and only pretended to sip it.

A young woman with a platinum wig and a short tight red dress slid onto the stool next to him.

"Buy a girl a drink?" she asked.

"Why? Don't you have any money?" Remo turned to look at her, his dark eyes drilling into hers. She leaned closer to him on her chair.

"I'll buy you one," she said. She waved at the bartender and fished a twenty-dollar bill from her sequined red handbag.

The bartender stood in front of them.

"Usual?" he asked the blonde. She nodded. "And you?" he asked Remo.

"Got any bottled water?" Remo asked.

"No."

"I'll coast with this one," Remo said. The bartender brought back a light tan mixture in a glass, put it in front of the blonde and reached for Remo's money.

"No," Remo said. "She's buying."

"That right, Jonelle?" the bartender said.

"Right, right," the blonde said.

The bartender glared at Remo, then said to the girl, "All right. This one's on the house."

Jonelle put her left hand on her drink and her right hand on Remo's thigh. He took the hand off his thigh and put it back on her own leg.

"How's business?" he asked.

"So-so."

"I would have said this town was the pits for a working girl," Remo said. "Who could afford you?"

"I was hoping you could," Jonelle said.

"Maybe we can work something out," Remo said. He pretended to sip his water and put his left hand onto the base of her neck. Next to the long muscle running down the right side of her neck, he found a bunch of nerves and tapped on them rapidly with his fingertips.

"Ooooooh," she said. "What are you doing?"

"Nice name, Jonelle," he said.

"Not my real name," the girl said. "Ooooooh," she exclaimed again. Her breath was coming faster.

"No?" Remo said. "I'm surprised. You look like a Jonelle I used to know. You were telling me about business."

"Getting better the last few weeks," she said. "More people in town. Maybe the new mayor's got something to do with it."

"The mayor have a piece of you?" Remo asked.

"Ooooooh. I don't know. My boyfriend is kind of close to him."

"For boyfriend, read pimp?" Remo asked.

"Ooooooh. You might say that."

Remo transferred his hand to the left side of her neck. He felt her throat tingle as if she were being massaged with a trickle charge of electricity.

"Who's your boyfriend?" Remo asked.

A heavy hand fell over his hand. Jonelle winced as the hand squeezed. Remo turned to see a large man with bushy red hair and an open-necked sports shirt standing behind them.

"I am," the man said. He tried to squeeze harder, with his hand, but he found his hand off the girl's neck and back at his side.

Jonelle got up from the bar and walked quickly away.

"Any more questions?" the pimp asked Remo.

"Yeah," Remo said. "You ever drink this water?"

"What kinda question is that?" the pimp asked.

"Never mind," Remo said. "I'll try something easier. Do you pay off the mayor for protection?"

"I think that's one question too many, pal," the big man said.

"And one answer too few," Remo said. He reached out and took the pimp's right wrist in his left hand and dragged him to the bar. The pain felt like a saw cutting through his flesh and bone and the pimp gasped and allowed himself to be placed on the stool.

"That's easy," Remo said in his ear. "Smile. People are watching us."

The pimp looked around and forced an agonized smile toward the other end of the bar. He looked back when Remo tightened the hold on his wrist.

"Question by me: Do you pay the mayor for protection? Answer by you: I think that's one question too many, pal. Now, we try again. Do you pay the mayor for protection?" Remo squeezed to signal the end of the question.

"Yes, yes, yes," the pimp gasped.

"Do all the pimps?"

"If they want to keep operating."

Remo released the man's wrist. "Thank you and good day," he said. Before leaving the bar, he picked up Jonelle's change and carried it to the booth at the end of the bar where she was sitting. He put a fresh hundred dollar bill on top of it before giving it back to her. She looked at the money, then up at him.

"Some other time?" she said.

"Count on it," Remo said.

Back at his hotel room, Remo called Smith.

"I'm in Bay City," he said.

"And?" Smith asked.

"The mob's coming in," Remo said. "This new mayor, Rocco something, looks like he's giving the town away to the goons."

"I see," Smith said blandly.

Remo was surprised at Smith's lack of reaction.

"Yeah. It looks like he's getting a rakeoff on the numbers and he's got a piece of the hooker action in town. And the joint is crawling with guys that look like they belong in a laundry at San Quentin."

"Good," said Smith.

"Good?" Remo said. "What's good? You want me to hit this Rocco what's-his-face?"

"No," Smith said quickly. "No. Don't do that. Leave things alone. You and Chiun should just go on vacation. You've been working hard lately."

"Wait a minute," Remo said. "You're telling us to go on vacation because we've been working hard?"

"Forget I said that," Smith said. "But you might as well go away for a few days until I need you."

"Thank you, Smitty. I'm almost ready to believe you're human."

"Don't get carried away," Smith said. "And going on vacation doesn't mean that you have to try to spend all the government's money in one day."

After Remo hung up, he looked at Chiun, who was staring through the motel window at the large backup of rush hour traffic along the Jersey City highway.

"I don't understand Smitty," Remo said.

"What is to understand? The man is a lunatic. He was always a lunatic," Chiun said. "He wants us to go away?"

"On vacation."

Chiun shook his head. The small white puffs of hair at his temples shook gently.

"No," Chiun said. "That is what he said. But what he wants is for us merely to leave this place."

"I don't need much encouragement," Remo said.

Chiun looked up, his face suddenly exuberant. "They say-

"I know. They say Persia is nice this time of year and the melons are in full bloom or whatever melons are full of. Well, forget it. We're not going to Persia."

"Where are we going?" Chiun asked.

"We're going fishing," Remo said.

"Pfaaaaah," said Chiun.

CHAPTER FOUR

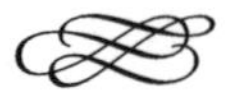

When other members of his engineering school graduating class went out to build bridges and highways and spaceships, Samuel Arlington Gregory got a job with a handgun designer.

It was a career the twenty-three-year-old Gregory had been pointing toward ever since he had been a little boy and had spent the summers at his grandfather's farm near Buffalo.

Grampa Gregory was a tall man with muscled, sloping shoulders who gave the impression of being built out of tanned weathered leather.

His friends called him Moose and everybody in the small New York town was his friend, because that was the way Grampa Gregory lived his life. He went to church every Sunday and stayed awake. When a neighbor's barn burned down, he was the first to volunteer to help build a new one. He lived by his word and they said in the town that Moose Gregory's handshake could be put into the bank and it'd draw interest.

He was the most middle-American of middle-Americans, except for one idiosyncrasy. He believed that the day was not far off when the Indians who had once owned and inhabited that section of the country would rise up to try to take it back.

"When that day comes, Sammy," he would tell his only grandson, "we've got to be ready. A man's got to defend what's his. You know what I mean?"

"The Indians aren't going to fight with us, Grampa," the eight-year-old Samuel Arlington Gregory would say. "There aren't even many Indians left."

Moose shook his head at the small boy. "Don't let them fool you. They're out there." He looked around and leaned close to the boy. "The Mafia's working with them this time. They want the Indians to get it back because they'll be able to take it away from them easier. You know what I mean?"

And young Sam Gregory would nod, even though he wasn't sure what his grandfather meant by the Mafia. The boy had come to hate his summers on the farm. He went because his parents made him go, expecting that it would help build character in the young boy. All summer long, he worked for his keep. He tried to spend as much of that worktime as possible around the house helping his grandmother, a warm, cuddly woman whose smell was redolent of biscuits and dumplings and eggs and bacon. His grandfather frightened him with his talk of Indians and the Mafia, and also just because he was a big man in a big man's world. The boy did not take any solace in the knowledge that one day he would be a man and join that man's world. It was his nature to be frightened by the future, just as he was frightened of his grandfather.

And never was he more frightened than on Saturday afternoons during the summer when Moose Gregory would take two rifles, a 30.06 and a .22 caliber, down from a rack in the lightless wood-paneled living room of the farmhouse. The young boy would trail his grandfather out into the woods that ringed the 240-acre farm and that stretched, as dark as pitch, for miles in each direction. No flicker of sunlight seemed ever to have reached the forest floor.

The old man, carrying both rifles under his left arm and a bag of bottles in his right hand, would stop at a small clearing deep in the woods. He would stack a dozen bottles in one end of the clearing, on stumps, in the fork of trees, on an old hollow log. Then he would come back and direct young Sam to strip the .22 rifle and clean it. Sam would take the rifle apart, clean it with an oiled rag his grandfather kept in a waterproof pouch, and then put it back together, all under the old man's intense gaze.

Only then would Grampa Gregory give Sam bullets, .22 caliber long rifle shells. The boy slipped the shells into the ammunition reservoir of the repeating rifle, and then at his grandfather's direction fired at the bottles.

Generally he missed, and his grandfather would kick dirt, and tell him with a chill in his voice, "When the Indians and the Mafia come, you're not going to be much help, boy."

Sam would reload and try again, usually with no better results.

"You're trying too hard," the old man said. "You're holding that rifle like it's poisoned and you're afraid it's catching. You have to make it feel like part of your body. Like it belongs to you and you love it. Like this." And the old man would raise his 30.06 and, seemingly without sighting, pull off a half dozen shots that would scatter bottles and glass chips ten feet high in the air. Young Sam Gregory hated the sharp report of the guns; he hated the sight of the bottles flying; and even though he did try, he could never get the hang of it.

The old man and the boy would stay in the woods until the pocket of his grandfather's red plaid mackinaw, in which he kept a boxful of .22 caliber shells, was empty and then they would trudge back to the house.

And occasionally, the old man would notice that the boy was upset over his failure and he would clap a large hand on his shoulder and say, "Some people ain't maybe cut out for firing guns. But that doesn't mean you aren't worth a lot. Everybody can do good in the world in their own way. That's why we were put here." And young Sam would hope that was the end of the target practice, but next Saturday, the old man would reach up to the living room rack and take down the rifles again for their regular foray into the woods.

As he grew older, the boy began to read all the books he could find on rifles and handguns. With money he earned he bought himself a target rifle. He never learned his grandfather's secret of making the rifle feel a part of his body, but he learned to shoot by using telescopic sights and mechanical tricks. He developed a gadget that would automatically alter the weight of the trigger pull on a gun, so that even if he did jerk it while firing, it would be too late to have any effect because the bullet was already on its way. Later, he devised a wrist brace to help a marksman hold a heavy handgun without wavering or swaying. He made his own guns.

And all the while, he hated guns and shooting, but something in the back of his mind kept him at it, because he wanted to prove something to his grandfather.

After engineering school, the first thing he invented was a new kind of cartridge, whose slug fragmented. However, unlike other fragmentation shells that scattered in all directions, the Gregory shell fragmented in a steady predictable pattern so that when fired at any target, one of the pieces of slug was sure to take the target down.

It was years since his grandmother had died and Grampa Gregory was living alone on the farm, still working it himself, when Sam showed up one weekend with a box of his new shells and challenged him to a shooting match.

The old man was now in his seventies. He was still big and strong looking, but to young Sam, the smell of death seemed to be on him, the feeling that this giant oak of a man had already been splintered by life's lightning and was just waiting to die.

Wordlessly the two men walked out into the woods. The only concession to the change in age was that on this trip young Sam Gregory carried the bottles.

He set the bottles on the ground, fifty yards from where his grandfather stood. He was careful to space them far enough apart so that none of his new fragmentation shells would take out two bottles at once.

He walked back to his grandfather and started to load the .22 rifle.

"Hold on, son. You ain't gonna clean that piece first?" his grandfather said.

The younger man nodded and took the weapon apart, cleaned it and reassembled it.

He loaded it and stood next to his grandfather.

"Which six you want, Grampa?" he asked.

"I'll take the ones on the left," the old man said. He moved back and sat down on a tree stump, then lifted his rifle to his shoulder and pulled off six rapid shots. Six bottles shattered and the old man looked at his grandson.

"Not bad, Grampa," Sam Gregory said. From a standing position, he raised his rifle and squeezed off six rapid shots. The last six bottles shattered.

When he turned to look at his grandfather, the old man had a strange look on his face.

"I guess you're ready for those Indians and that Mafia now," the old man said softly. Even as he spoke, his face was turning a pained pasty white. His rifle dropped from the crook of his arm. He tried to raise both hands to his chest, but before he could, the old man fell backward off the tree stump. He was dead.

Back at the munitions plant, Sam continued working on the fragmentation bullets, altering and modifying them for a large range of guns from rifles to pistols. Then he devised a new type of handgun, built for the fragmentation shells, and coupled with a new scope of his own design. The telescopic sight contained a series of lenses, mounted in such a way that the gun could be used at arm's length, and the intensified-light image on the scope would be as clear as watching a picture on a miniature television receiver. On the scope's ground glass, around the image of the target, were a series of rings that corresponded to the approximate distance from the target. At 100 yards, if the target was somewhere in the center ring, the frag shell was certain to bring it down. At fifty yards, the target object could be anywhere within the two center rings and the shooter would be certain of hitting it. At twenty-five yards, the target could be anywhere in the scope, and the fragmentation bullets, now redesigned out of a softer metal that did more damage on impact, would be guaranteed to kill.

It was literally a gun that could not miss, and when Gregory had refined the design, he did two things. First, he resigned from the weapons company. Second, he patented the scope and the bullets and the handgun.

Soon after, he sent specifications of it to the Pentagon. Four months later, after signing a twenty-million-dollar contract to produce the guns for the Army, Sam Gregory was a rich man.

And, he realized increasingly as time went on, a bored one.

At his estate in Elberon, New Jersey, he tinkered with the design of other weapons, but his mind was not really on it.

He thought often of those days in the woods with his grandfather. Even at the end, he had not been able to beat the old man honestly in a shooting match. Was there anything else? The old man had often talked about doing good in the world, and that was the way he had tried to live his life. Maybe, just maybe, Sam Gregory thought, he might just be able to do more good than his grandfather had done.

One day, coming back from New York where he had seen his tax lawyer, he ran into a monumental traffic tieup coming out of the Holland Tunnel in Jersey City. To avoid the traffic, he had turned off the highway, and found himself wandering along the streets of Bay City.

All Sam Gregory knew about Bay City was that it was a waterfront town that had fallen on hard times. In the old days, his munitions plant often had delivered goods to dockside for shipment to Army posts overseas, but all that business in Bay City had stopped years before.

Trying to get through the town, he made a wrong turn and found himself on River Street, the long thoroughfare that fronted the city's old decaying piers. Up ahead of him, near the curb, he saw a black chauffeured limousine. That surprised him. Bay City was not the kind of community for chauffeured limousines. He saw a man get out of the back seat of the car, flanked by two ugly-looking bodyguards.

"A greaseball," he said to himself and pulled to the curb to watch. The man was Mafia. He knew it. He could tell.

And down the block he saw another. And around the corner, another.

Sam Gregory's mind was clicking as he drove through the town and when he saw the small office of the *Bay City Bugle,* he went inside and bought copies of each paper for the last six months.

When he took them home and read them, he realized what had happened.

Somehow, an outsider, Rocco Nobile, had come into the town, gotten himself installed as mayor and was now turning the city over to the Mafia.

Suddenly, Sam Gregory wasn't bored anymore. His grandfather had told him so often to do good, and he now had found the good thing to do, the thing that would give his life meaning and purpose.

He would drive the Mafia from Bay City.

A touch of asthma, a sinus condition and a generally runny nose had kept Sam Gregory out of the Army, but even without military experience he knew that he needed a battle plan and soldiers to carry it out if he were to win his war against the Mafia.

It took him two weeks to get his army together.

There was Mark Tolan. He was a brooding, muscular, dark-haired man who had been court-martialed in Vietnam for proving the no-miss capability of the Gregory Sur-Shot handgun, primarily against women and children. He had tried to call Gregory as a defense witness at his court-martial, apparently on the unique legal theory that if he could prove how easy it was to kill with that gun, the court-martial board would understand why he had plugged two dozen women and children. Gregory had appeared, but Tolan, a career sergeant, was still thrown out of service. He had been working for the last four years in a drive-in restaurant.

The second member of the team was Al Baker whom Gregory had met one night in a New York restaurant. Baker had told him that he was a member of the Mafia who had fled the organization and lived, and offered to organize Gregory's weapons factory if he had any union problems. He had given Gregory his card which Gregory had saved, but had never known why. He remembered his grandfather's worries about the Mafia and would never have anything to do with anyone in the mob. But now...now that he was fighting the mob, a man with Baker's connections and knowledge would be a definite asset, particularly since he had long ago left the mob. He did not know that Al Baker was a small time numbers runner whose closest connection with the Mafia had been seeing *The Godfather* twenty-three times and thereafter practicing talking like Marlon Brando.

The final member of the team was a former actor who had taken to writing Gregory a lot of letters after an article about the gun designer had appeared in a national magazine. The letters had quoted Shakespeare a lot and praised Gregory's inventions and prayed, forsooth, that the weapons would only be used on the scum of the world which deserved that kind of end. Gregory liked the writer's literary style — it was the fanciest thing he had ever seen — and had started to correspond with him. The actor's name was Nicholas Lizzard. He was an emaciated six-foot-five. He carried a doctor's leather bag with him, in which he carried makeup for disguises. His skill was such that, fully made up, he could mask his height and look barely six-feet-four.

All four men now sat around poolside at Sam Gregory's Elberon estate.

Gregory was drawing a chart. He listed himself as the commander in a big pencil-drawn box. Below that he had three other smaller pencil-drawn boxes. In them he put the army's names: Mark Tolan, Al Baker, Nicholas Lizzard. He drew lines connecting all the boxes.

"This is our table of organization," he said. He looked around the table. Nicholas Lizzard was pouring a refill of iced Vodka into a tall water glass. Mark Tolan was sighting down the barrel of an unloaded Gregory Sur-Shot at a concrete duck on the far side of the swimming pool. Only Al Baker was looking at the chart. He was rubbing his hands together nervously.

"Nice table of organization," he said. "Like we had in the Mafia, when I was a soldier, before I managed to escape with my life. Want me to tell you about it?"

"Not right now," Gregory said. He turned toward Mark Tolan. "Stop that," he said. Tolan was staring down the sights of the Gregory Sur-Shot at a point halfway between Sam Gregory's eyes, squeezing the trigger. Behind the butt of the gun and his hand, his face was impassive, darkly brooding. He gave no sign that he had heard Gregory, but he turned quietly in his chair and began to draw a bead on birds flying overhead. Under his breath, Gregory could hear him saying softly, "Bang. Bang."

Gregory looked at Nicholas Lizzard, who was just finishing his glass of Vodka, and casting eyes at the bottle. As he reached for it, Gregory got it first, and set it on the flagstone patio under his feet. He leaned over and snatched the Gregory Sur-Shot from Mark Tolan's hands. Tolan wheeled in his chair, his face red with hate, his cold eyes narrowed with rage. It was the face of a homicidal maniac, Gregory realized, and he decided that Mark Tolan would be the number one captain in his war against the Mafia.

"Now listen, you three," Gregory said. "You know what's wrong with you?"

"Yeah, we're poor," Baker said.

"No. Like me, you're bored," Gregory said. "You've got nothing to do in your life. You, Baker, you're busy fooling around with unions, and you, Mark, you're a short-order cook in a quickie restaurant, and you, Lizzard, you're an actor without parts."

"Man of many parts," Lizzard said, somewhat thickly. "Many parts."

Tolan laughed derisively.

"Hark," said Lizzard. "I do believe that Jack the Ripper chuckles."

The thin actor had his chin on his hands on the table. Tolan growled and lunged across the table with his own hands, reaching for Lizzard's throat. Lizzard recoiled. Tolan missed. He looked toward the gun in Gregory's lap.

"Stop it, you two. Stop it," Gregory said.

"Yeah," Baker said. "The Mafia's got more discipline than this. We act like this, we ain't got no chance. You wanna know how the Mafia woulda done this?"

"What do you know about the Mafia, you clown?" Tolan said. Gregory realized they were the first words Tolan had said since arriving, except for "Bang, bang" under his breath.

"Enough. Enough," Gregory said. "You see what I mean? You men, all of us, we're so bored, we don't have anything better to do than to pick on each other. Picky. Picky."

"Dicky doo," said Tolan.

Gregory ignored him. He pointed at each of the three men, in turn, with his Eberhard Faber Mongol 482 #1 yellow pencil.

"But that's all over now. We've got something to live for. We're going to live big lives. They're going to know we were here. We're going to live huge."

"Ah, life, its sweetness challenges me," said Lizzard, who had returned his head to his hands and was drifting off to sleep.

"How we gonna live?" Baker said. "I'm giving up a good job union organizing."

"Money's not your worry anymore," Gregory said. "We're an army and we're a well-financed army. And the enemy is the Mafia in Bay City. We're going after them, boys."

"Good," said Tolan. "Kill 'em all. Blow their eyes out. Shoot their brains all over the street. Gut shoot them so they die slow. Fill them up with compressed air and let them blow up. Skin them alive before we shoot them. Toss their guts in the street. Set fire to their intestines."

Lizzard retched. Baker covered his mouth with his hand so he wouldn't throw up on the table.

"Well, something like that," Gregory said. He pointed with his pencil at the table of organization. "This is it. Our army. We need a name."

"What for?" said Baker nervously. He did not want anyone to find out he was connected with these loonies.

"If we don't have a name, how will we get fan mail?" Tolan said.

"That ain't funny," said Baker.

"We need a name because we want them to know who's after them. We want them to fear the dark," Gregory said. "To know that each step could be their last. To know that each person they pass on the street might live only to see them die. We want them to be afraid as they have made others afraid. That's why," He pointed with his pencil. "That's why we need a name." To emphasize the point, he grabbed the pencil in both hands and snapped it. He looked at the broken piece in his right hand, then looked around the table. Tolan was looking up toward the sky, pointing his index finger at birds, going "Bang, bang" under his breath. Lizzard seemed asleep. All Gregory could see was the thinning hair on the top of his pink head. Baker was looking around nervously as if expecting the backyard to be raided.

"That's it," Gregory said. He held up the rubber-tipped end of the pencil.

"From here on in, I'm The Eraser." He waved the eraser over his head. "And you're...you're all...The Rubout Squad."

"Who do I kill first?" asked Tolan.

"Can I have the Vodka back now?" asked Lizzard without raising his head.

"You was talking about us getting paid," Baker said. "How much and when?"

"We're going to get them all," said Gregory. "The goons and the gunsels and the ginzos. And most of all, that corrupting mayor, Rocco Nobile."

CHAPTER FIVE

"THE CLIMATE IS VERY GOOD HERE," Mayor Rocco Nobile said into the telephone.

"It's good here too," came back the gruff voice. "It was in the eighties yesterday and we ain't getting no rain at all."

Nobile looked away and sighed. "I mean the business climate," he said.

"Oh yeah. That. Okay. Well, we was talking about it yesterday and everybody kinda thinks it's a good idea, moving and all."

"Sure," Nobile said. "Centralize your operation. It's just good business."

"That's the word they used yesterday too. Centralize. They said it was like General Motors, they don't go building cars everyplace, except they stay in that grubby frigging Detroit."

"Right. And what's good for General Motors is good for you," Nobile said.

"Exactly. Count on us, Rocco."

"Okay. Take care." Nobile hung up the telephone in his apartment and sighed again. He had been on the telephone all morning to the West Coast suggesting to certain independent businessmen that their business operations might be more soundly run in Bay City. He described the beautiful location, just minutes away from the New York metropolitan area, the world's prime market for everything legal and illegal. He pointed out the city's natural harbor, which he was now having cleaned up to reopen the channels and allow ships to move in and out from foreign countries, more or less freely. There would be, he emphasized, no federal money involved in the harbor cleanup and therefore no federal personnel hovering around, watching things that didn't concern them.

He had held this discussion before with many other independent businessmen and all had told him they might be interested once he had proven he could get control of Bay City. Now he had it and he could deliver it to them.

On his way to his office, Rocco Nobile felt satisfied that within the next few weeks more of the vacant lofts along River Street would soon have new tenants, new and thriving businesses.

Nobile arrived at his office at 9:15 A.M. in the old dilapidated City Hall, where he had specifically rejected a suggestion that the building be repainted. The last thing he wanted was to give some kind of signal that might drift to the outside world that things were changing in Bay City. The city had, for years, been ignored by the world and the press and he would be happy to keep it that way. He only wished the harbor cleanup work could be done at night so no one would notice that it was underway.

At 11:30 A.M., he met with his five-member City Commission, three of whose members had voted to install him as mayor and whose other two members had abstained. They talked about the impending city budget, about which Mayor Nobile knew nothing and cared less and they talked about the prospect of payroll cuts and Nobile told them to do whatever they wanted. When the meeting was over, he asked the three councilmen who had voted him into office to stay for a few minutes and when the two abstentions had left the room, Nobile handed the councilmen fat envelopes filled with cash.

"More where that came from, fellas," he said.

"Good," said Walter Fingal O'Flaherty Wills Wilde. "Keep it coming."

Outside the mayor's office, the three councilmen found reasons to burrow themselves into corners so they could look into the envelopes and make sure they hadn't been handed coupons from the newspaper instead of cash.

At noon, Rocco Nobile began to look through the day's mail, a boring task which annoyed him because all the good mail was never sent by mail. It was hand-delivered to his apartment at the Bay City Arms.

He looked quickly through the stack of letters. Employee unions, state environmental agencies, federal bureaus, fan mail. One letter was unopened. There was a lump in the middle of the brown envelope and on the outside his name had been printed in ink along with a warning: *personal. confidential.*

The letter was handwritten on lined yellow paper. It was printed in block letters. It read:

MAYOR NOBILE. YOU ARE A BLOT UPON THE FACE OF AMERICA. THE ERASER RUBS OUT BLOTS. YOUR TIME IS COMING SOON.

It was signed: *THE ERASER.*

And Scotch-taped to the bottom of the letter was half of a broken pencil, the eraser end.

Nobile scratched his head under the blue-black hair and, as was customary, looked at his fingertips as he withdrew his hand. Then he read the letter again.

On his private telephone line, he dialed a number he had never called before but had committed to memory. He did not know who was on the other end of the line.

When the dry voice answered, he said simply, "I'm in trouble."

There was this little store off Canal Street in New York City that sold pure silk blouses from Hong Kong at half the price you could buy them anywhere else, so Ruby Gonzalez was going to go there and spend some time. But first she had to get out of Bay City, which was ugly.

She wanted to get to the store early so she had no time to waste.

She walked around the back of the Bay City Arms apartment building. It was a warm day and Ruby wore a white halter top and black slacks. Her coffee-with-milk skin seemed a perfect middle ground between the light and dark of her clothing.

There was a ramp behind the building leading to an underground garage, and whistling lightly and swinging her purse, Ruby walked down the ramp. It was cool and airless under the building. Forty cars were parked in numbered slots and she had no trouble picking out the black Cadillac with the New Jersey MG — meaning municipal government — license plates which belonged to Mayor Rocco Nobile.

She stood behind the Cadillac for a moment, looking around. There was no one else in the garage. She rooted into her purse and found a large Idaho baking potato. She bent over and jammed it into the end of the exhaust pipe.

It could just as easily have been a bomb.

As she was walking from the garage, a man came out the door at the far end of the building.

Ruby made a sharp turn and walked rapidly toward him.

"Hold the door," she called. She smiled at him.

He held the door open for her as she brushed by him.

"Thanks," she said.

"Have a nice day," he said.

She waited until the heavy metal door swung shut behind her, then got her bearings and went to the elevator.

Inside she pressed the top-floor button. When the door opened, she was in a carpeted hall, facing four doors. One of the central doors had potted plants on each side of it. That would be the main entrance to Rocco Nobile's apartment.

Ruby fished in her purse and found a thin strip of steel, the size of a credit card.

She listened at the door at the far left end of the hall. There was no sound from inside. She slipped the thin strip of metal under the wood molding of the door frame near the lock. She pressed hard, and felt the lock slip open. She pulled the door out a half-inch to satisfy herself there was no other lock. She pushed the door closed and removed the metal strip, quietly relocking the door.

She did the same thing at the door at the far right side of the hall.

Then she rode back down on the elevator.

In the lobby, she waved at the doorman who waved back. She smiled at him as he opened the door for her. Breezily, she walked across the street and got behind the wheel of her white Lincoln Continental.

So far, she thought, it was a joke.

She kept her eyes on the front door of the apartment building, occasionally checking behind her in the rearview mirror.

Fifteen minutes later, she saw the mayor's black limousine turning the corner. Ruby picked up a grocery bag off the back seat of the car. In her mind, it could very easily have contained a submachine gun.

She got out of her car and walked across the street just as the mayor's car, bucking and puffing, pulled up to the front door of the Bay City Arms.

As she drew close to the front entrance, the door opened and a man she assumed was the mayor stepped outside. Another man followed behind him. The mayor smiled at Ruby. The bodyguard scowled, then held the door to the rear seat open for Rocco Nobile.

The car sputtered. Ruby walked toward it. If she had carried a machine gun, she would simply have taken it out now and used it.

Instead, she said to the bodyguard still standing next to the car, "There's something stuck in your exhaust pipe."

He looked at her suspiciously.

She smiled and pointed to the rear of the car. "The exhaust pipe," she said. "Something's stuck in it."

The man growled. Ruby shrugged. She turned away from the building. Rocco Nobile saw her and smiled and gave her a small wave. She waved back.

The potato was removed from the exhaust and the mayor's car had driven away, before Ruby drove her own car out of Bay City toward the Holland Tunnel to New York.

She stopped to use a telephone in a booth alongside the roadway.

"Doctor Smith?" she said.

"Yes," answered Harold W. Smith.

"Ruby. That mayor got no security at all."

"As bad as that?" Smith asked.

"Yeah," Ruby said. "I coulda put a bomb under his car and no one would have noticed. I got into his building with no trouble at all. I slipped two of the locks into his apartment. And when he came out to go to work, I walked right up to him and I coulda blown him away. His bodyguards are hopeless."

Smith sighed on the other end of the phone.

"Thank you, Ruby."

"I think if you got some reason to want to keep that man alive, you better send in somebody. Send in the dodo. He can do it."

"All right, Ruby," Smith said. "When will you be back?"

Ruby pictured those half-price silk blouses in her mind. "Take a few hours," she lied. "I'm having me some car trouble."

CHAPTER SIX

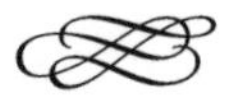

THE FORTY-FOOT LONG wooden boat drifted aimlessly through the Atlantic Ocean. It had dieseled out at dawn from Montauk on the eastern tip of Long Island, only forty miles away, but its direction was northeast, and when the boat's motors were turned off, it lay in 450 feet of water 120 miles due east of Manhattan.

Remo and Chiun sat atop a wooden locker on the back deck. Remo had peeled off his usual black T-shirt and was wearing only his black chinos and a pair of white leather running shoes with black diagonal stripes across the top. Chiun wore a white brocaded kimono which Remo estimated weighed at least fifteen pounds.

Over his bare chest, Remo had put a thick leather harness, cut like a short vest. Hooked below his belt was a padded metal gimbal, a cup-like device that looked as if it was designed to hold a flagpole.

"I do not understand this," Chiun said. He had said it half a dozen times on the three-hour trip out into the ocean and Remo ignored it as he had the earlier five times.

He watched the rear of the boat as Mickey, the mate, cut up herring and threw slices out into the oily chum slick the boat was trailing through the water. Two-inch-thick fishing poles angled out from the side of the boat, their heavy nylon lines pulled out at almost 90-degree angles from the perpendicular.

"Why do you want to kill a fish that isn't doing anything to you and that you do not eat?" Chiun said. "What did a shark ever do to you?"

"I'm getting even for *Jaws,*" Remo said. "That shark scared a hundred million people."

"Is that shark here?" Chiun asked.

"That was a mechanical shark. Plastic and metal."

"And you are going to get your revenge by attacking a flesh and blood shark?" Chiun said.

"Absolutely. I kill thirty people last week and you don't care. I come out here to kill a shark and you get all bent out of shape. I don't understand you, Chiun."

Remo pointed toward Mickey. The big husky blond mate leaned over the rear of the boat toward the water. "Come on, sveethots," he called out softly. "Mickey is here to kill all you bastards." He shook his fist at the quiet water and fingered the knife in the leather scabbard at his waist.

"You should have got *him* for training," Remo said.

"At least he has the right attitude," Chiun said, "even if he does waste it on a poor harmless fish."

Remo started to answer but there was a screaming whistle as the line began to unreel off one of the rods. Even though the reel was on full drag and a grown man would have had trouble pulling line off it, this line was whistling out at top speed.

"Hit," Mickey yelled out. "Hit."

Remo jumped up and ran to the fishing rod. He lifted it from its holder and pushed it into the metal cup he wore on the belt across his groin. He fastened two leather clips from the leather vest to the sides of the pole. He was now securely fastened to the rod and reel. If they went overboard, so did he.

As they had motored out to the fishing grounds that morning, Mickey had told Remo, "A lot of people think that's so they don't get hurt, but that's bullshit. We clip them to the rod and reel so they know if they drop it, they go over with it."

"You lose a lot of fishermen that way?" Remo asked.

"Frig 'em. Anybody lets a shark slide deserves what he gets."

Remo moved to the stern of the boat and began reeling in the line. He knew the delicate point of the operation — the weak link in this hookup between man and fish was the thin nylon line that connected them. The fish had the power to snap the line and so did Remo and the skill was in bringing the fish into the boat without breaking the line and losing the fish.

The boat rocked back and forth in the water on the soft Atlantic waves. As it rocked backward, away from the fish, Remo held the pole taut. Then as the boat rocked forward, Remo reeled down quickly to take up slack in the line. Slowly, foot by foot, he was bringing the fish in closer to the boat.

"Can you see it?" Remo asked Mickey, who stood alongside him, his gray-green eyes squinted, scanning the water for the sign of fins or a telltale glimpse of the shark.

"Don't know. Keep reeling." He paused, then whistled. "Son of a bitch. Look at that."

A dorsal fin cut through the water toward the boat. The fin stuck three feet up out of the water.

"It's a great white!" Mickey yelled. "The big bastard. Reel, you sucker. Reel in that line."

There was no pressure now on the line as Remo reeled. The fish swam toward the boat faster than Remo could pull in the slack line.

"Chiun, come look at this," Remo called.

"Away with you," Chiun said in disgust.

The fish was only fifteen feet from the boat when it surged. Its giant head came up out of the water, its knife-like nose cutting above the bubbly white-green foam, its round marble eyes staring insanely at Remo on the side of the boat. The shark opened its mouth and Remo looked down into the yawning tan-and-pink chasm, at row after row of needle triangular teeth. The mouth stretched two feet across from side to side and, involuntarily, Remo leaned backward and the fish dropped back into the water and passed under the boat.

Mickey pushed Remo toward the stern of the boat so Remo could pass the line around under the boat to prevent it from snagging under the old vessel's hull and breaking.

"How big?" Remo asked.

"A giant," Mickey said. "A monster. A Jaws. Keep reeling."

Remo got around to the right rear end of the boat just in time to see the shark move up to the surface of the water and angle sharply to the right. The shark was at least twenty feet long.

"A great white!" Mickey yelled. "I told you! Do whatever you want, but don't let him break that line." He was unclipping a ten-foot-long steel harpoon from its rack under the gunwhale. "Cap'n," he yelled. "Wake up."

"Hah?" came a voice from the cockpit, twelve feet above the deck.

"Great white," Mickey yelled. "Start the engines."

"Hah?"

"Shit," Mickey cursed softly. He screamed. "Start the frigging engines!" To Remo, he said, "Two tons if he's an ounce. Don't let him snap that line. When he comes close again, I'll get this harpoon in him."

"It's a great white," Remo called over his shoulder toward Chiun.

"An improbably named species," Chiun sniffed.

The fish was racing parallel to the boat now, along its left side. Remo saw that if the shark made a quick turn in toward the boat, his line could get hopelessly hung up on the cleats or hardware on the front of the boat and snap. He started working his way forward along the side of the boat. He tripped over Chiun's feet.

"Watch your feet, Chiun," he growled.

"Watch your mouth, great white thing," Chiun said.

Remo hopped up onto the railing. There was still slack in the line so there was no danger of his being jerked overboard and Remo walked along the railing until he was in the front of the boat. The shark dove under the water and then swerved right, passing in front of the boat. Remo kept reeling up slack.

"Good move, sveethot," Mickey said as he came up behind Remo, the long harpoon in his hand. He hooked it to a half-inch-thick nylon rope, which was fastened to three barrels. If the harpoon got into the shark and he pulled out the heavy line, the barrels were supposed to make it harder for him to sound, to drive straight down, because their buoyancy would keep fighting him back upward.

"Come on, you sucker, come back," Mickey yelled at the fish, which was passing from left to right across the front of the boat, barely visible as it cruised just under the water sixty yards away. As if he had heard the mate, the shark turned and raced toward the prow of the boat. Remo heard the motors of the boat start behind him.

The giant shark raced straight toward the bow of the boat. Remo could almost feel the anger in the giant fish's body. When the shark was only fifteen feet away, Mickey raised the harpoon to his right shoulder and fired. It bit into the flesh of the shark close behind the bullet head and the shark twitched and dropped below the surface of the water.

The barrels went skimming off the front of the deck boat.

"All right. You can cut your line now if you want," Mickey told Remo. The shark, racing toward the stern of the boat under the water, yanked the rope against the bow of the boat and it turned slowly in the water; and then the shark was speeding back toward Manhattan and the boat followed along behind him, the captain gunning the engines, trying to stay close enough to the shark so that the fish's strength wasn't pitted against the boat's weight, in which case the only casualty would be the half-inch-thick line connecting them.

Remo used his fingers to snap the nylon line on his fishing pole, as if it had been an overcooked strand of vermicelli. He stuck the pole into a rack alongside the gunwale and followed Mickey, who had gone to the stern to prepare another harpoon. If they could get another harpoon into the shark, they could slow him down by letting the weight of the boat drag on him. Until then, though, the rule was let him run.

"Fun, isn't it, Chiun?" Remo said.

Chiun fixed him with a chilling glance and folded his hands across his chest.

Mickey had the second harpoon assembled and Remo followed him to the front of the boat.

As the mate hooked another line to the harpoon, they suddenly felt the boat rock backward slightly, as if it had been caught in the wake of a large passing ship. Remo saw the blue-and-white nylon line which had been attached to the shark limply drop into the water.

"Shit, shit and triple shit," shouted Mickey. "The sucker snapped the line." He shook his fist out at the sea. The three barrels bobbed around on the surface of the water, still connected by the line to the shark. Then as if they had been attached to a falling mountain of rock, they dropped straight beneath the surface of the water. Remo and the mate stared for long seconds as the barrels disappeared, and then, as if they were corks released underwater, the barrels rose again, shooting eight feet up into the air, before hitting back down with a string of three slap splashes. Above their heads, the captain cut the engines.

"We lost it, Chiun," Remo called back.

"Good," said Chiun.

"You don't understand," Remo said. "It was a giant. A record, maybe."

"This fish was very important to you?"

"Yes."

"If you caught it, we would go back to our room before I am burned black by this malevolent sun?"

"Yes."

"I see," Chiun said.

Mickey nudged Remo. "He may come back. Sometimes they do."

The two men stood at the front of the boat, watching, their eyes circling, but the ocean was still.

"We're far away from the chum slick," Remo said.

"Makes no difference," the mate said. "When there's a great white around, the other sharks make themselves scarce."

Remo glanced back and noticed that Chiun had risen from his seat on the locker. He was standing at the rear of the boat. From behind, he appeared to be dipping his hands into the water. Mickey noticed him too.

"What's he doing?" the mate asked.

"Don't be surprised at anything," Remo said.

As they both looked toward the stern, they saw it. The giant shark came up to the surface of the water, directly behind the boat. He was only thirty feet away. He sped toward the boat at full speed.

Mickey ran toward the rear of the vessel.

"Chiun, look out," Remo called. He started back also. Chiun did not move.

The shark was upon the boat now and the vessel shuddered as the giant fish hit it at full speed. Remo could see the snout of the big beast rise above the gunwale as his teeth and mouth rammed the back of the boat. Chiun, instead of retreating, leaned further over toward the water.

Mickey grabbed another harpoon. Remo ran up behind Chiun. Before the two men reached him, the old Korean turned, an angelic smile of calm on his face.

"Now we go?" he said to Remo.

And behind him, the body of the great white shark rose slowly to the surface, floating, its eyes already glazed over with death. It was a full twenty-feet long and its tail fins fluttered feebly as it floated behind the boat, and then it slowly revolved onto its back and its white belly reflected the afternoon sunlight like a piece of metallic foil.

Mickey tossed the harpoon into the shark's belly and quickly secured the nylon rope to one of the rear cleats.

"I don't believe it," Remo said. "I've seen sharks with a bullet in their head live for hours."

"I have seen grasshoppers withstand cannon shot," Chiun said.

Remo said "How?"

"Because the cannon shot missed. The bullets in the shark's head missed. I do not miss."

"Got to bring him to side before he sinks," Mickey said. He began hauling the shark in closer to get another line around his tail. The captain came down from the top cabin to lend a hand.

"What happened to him?" the captain asked.

"Don't know, Cap," the mate answered.

"They don't just die for no reason," the captain said.

Mickey shrugged. "Got me," he said.

As the two men struggled to bring the shark in, Remo asked Chiun, "How'd you do that?"

"Do what?"

"Make him come. Then kill him."

"I called him with my fingers. It is really easy. If you had paid attention, you would have learned how. I think I taught that to you… yes, in your second month of training. Ten years ago. What? You mean to say you weren't listening?" Chiun looked at Remo quizzically. "Surely you must remember. It came right between my lecture on Ung poetry and the history of the House of Sinanju during the reign of the greatest Master, Wang. You do not remember this?"

"Don't be wise," Remo said. "You know I don't remember it. I slept through that month. How'd you kill him?"

"I hit him on the nose as I will hit you on the nose if we do not return immediately to our room."

Chiun climbed into the large deck chair, closed his eyes and pretended to nap.

Behind him, Remo heard someone swear.

He looked up to see Mickey and the captain leaning over the port side of the boat. When he joined them, he saw the faint trace of the great white's silvery-brown body slipping down through the waters toward the bottom of the ocean.

For a moment, Remo thought of jumping in after it to retrieve the line, but decided it would take too long. The shark would drop down to the bottom and within minutes other fish would begin eating away at the once-feared killer.

"Line broke," Mickey explained. "Damn."

When they got to shore, Chiun woke up and looked around.

"Where is the fish you wanted so badly?" he asked Remo.

"It got away," Remo said disconsolately.

"The big ones always do," Chiun said.

CHAPTER SEVEN

THE FISHING BOAT DROPPED Remo and Chiun off at a private dock jutting out into the ocean, before going back to the main marina where the mate and captain planned to tell everybody about the giant shark that just seemed to die of old age, but slipped the ropes and dropped to the bottom before they could boat it. In a town whose economic survival depended more and more on shark hunters and stories of great whites caught and almost caught, 90 percent of those who heard the story would smile and quietly consider it a lie. The other 10 percent would keep open minds. They themselves had run into great whites and they knew anything was possible.

When they walked across a hundred yards of sand dune and entered their motel room, Remo and Chiun found Dr. Harold W. Smith sitting in a chair. He was not watching television or reading a newspaper. He was simply sitting, as if sitting were an end in itself and he had worked hard to learn the technique of doing it well.

"You should've seen the shark we had, Smitty," Remo said. "Thirty feet." He spread his hands as wide apart as he could to illustrate.

Behind him, Chiun held up his right hand, with thumb and index finger separated by only about three inches. Silently, he mouthed the words to Smith, "A minnow."

"Yes, yes," Smith said. "I'm glad you've both enjoyed your vacation so much."

"Do I detect the past tense there?" Remo asked.

"Actually it was the present perfect," Smith said. "But past will do. I have an assignment."

"Bay City?"

"Yes," Smith said.

"I knew it. I knew it. I knew you were going to change your mind. I knew I should have hit that guy while we were there."

"Please, Remo," Chiun said. "Don't talk about hits. It makes you sound like some kind of killer."

"Sorry, Chiun," Remo said. He turned back to Smith. "All right, I'll finish it tomorrow."

"You don't understand," Smith said.

"What don't I understand?"

"You've got the job assignment wrong. I don't want to dispose of Mayor Nobile."

"What do you want me to do?"

"I want you to be his bodyguard. Protect him."

"From what? The FBI? An overdose of cavatelli? What?"

"I don't know from whom or from what. He got a threatening letter today from someone who called himself 'The Eraser.'"

Remo sprawled down on the bed and looked over at Smith. Chiun turned on the television set and pulled the vanity chair around so he was sitting six inches from the screen. A sports program was showing the full contact karate championships. Chiun turned off the set in disgust. He had hoped there would be an ice skating show on. He had fallen in love with one of the skaters. When he found out she was married to a football player, he watched football hoping the player would be killed and cursed defensive linemen for their inability to make him into a vegetable.

"'The Eraser?'" Remo said.

Smith nodded.

"Why should we care if Rocco Nobile gets himself knocked off by The Eraser or by anybody else for that matter? I told you he was turning that city over to the mob. What's it to us?" He put his hands behind his head and looked at the ceiling.

Smith cleared his throat. Chiun went into the bathroom to count the bars of soap. If there were extras, they would go into one of his trunks.

"Remo," Smith said, "a number of years ago the CIA had an agent in Europe named Wardell Pinkerton the Third."

"He must have been a winner," Remo said.

"He was. He was one of the best field agents the CIA ever had. Then he developed heart trouble and had to be moved out of active line duty. He came back to the States."

"And today, I believe, that man is a certified public accountant?" Smith looked at Remo in confusion but Remo was rewarded by Chiun's roar of laughter from the bathroom. They had been in New York City one evening to buy roasted chestnuts and they had happened onto a playhouse off the main theater district. The picture in the box office window illustrating the play was so appalling that they went inside to see it. It was a one-actor monologue with lines so deadly dull that half the audience was asleep in the first ten minutes. And when the actor delivered the line about the public accountant, Chiun could contain himself no longer. He leaped onto the stage and chased the actor off it. He was about to leave when he looked out and saw the seventy-five faces looking up at him from the darkness. He delivered one of the shortest of the Ung poems, and an hour later, when everybody in the audience was asleep, he and Remo left.

"Certified public accountant?" Smith said.

"Never mind," Remo said. "You had to be there. What happened to Pinker Waddington?"

"Wardell Pinkerton the Third. He retired to California. Then his wife and daughter were killed in an accident. He got bored and tired and started drinking too much and one day, he decided the only way to pull himself back together was to go back to work."

"So?"

"So he was recruited at the very highest levels of government for a secret mission. Wardell Pinkerton the Third vanished from the face of the earth."

"What has this got to do with me?" Remo asked. There were 266 pressed board tiles in the ceiling. Nineteen rows of fourteen each. Since Remo had never been able to multiply, he had counted each one of them.

"Well, precisely this," Smith said. "Wardell Pinkerton is Mayor Rocco Nobile."

Remo sat up in bed. "Say it again."

"Rocco Nobile, the mayor of Bay City, is Wardell Pinkerton the Third. He's a federal agent. He's working for us on this program, even though he doesn't know it is our operation. After he vanished from California, he had plastic surgery and then showed up again in Miami, where he used money to make mob connections. We were able to help him with that. We've been moving him around inside organized crime for five years. Then it was time to move. We sent him into Bay City to take over the town."

"But why? Why turn it over to thugs?"

"He has given an open invitation to organized crime to move its operations into Bay City. He's opening the piers so that contraband can move in and out easily. So drugs can flow freely. Mob interests are coming from all over the country. Cutting rooms and jewelry factories for stolen diamonds. Printing facilities for counterfeit stock certificates and securities. Major counting rooms for the nation's biggest illegal gambling operations."

"You still haven't told me why."

"Remo, he's turning it into a safe city, so we can get most of America's crime centralized there. And when we do, we're going to go in and shut it all down at once."

"I got it."

"Now you know why Rocco Nobile has to be kept alive. If anything happens to him now, the mob people will leave before we really get a chance to set them up. Remo, we want to get them all. We want to deal crime a blow that it might never recover from. That's why it's imperative you protect Rocco Nobile…er, Wardell Pinkerton."

"The Third," Remo said.

"Yes."

"All right," Remo said.

Smith said, "Of course, he doesn't know who you are or who you work for. He doesn't even know who he works for. He doesn't know CURE exists."

"Does he know we're coming?"

"He knows a government agent is coming to join his bodyguard staff, but you'll have to be discreet. You can't blow his cover. You've got to be a mob member protecting another mob member," Smith said.

"If I have to wear a pinky ring and a pinstripe suit, I quit," Remo said.

"Do the best you can." Smith stood up and picked up his briefcase from alongside the chair. He looked toward the closed bathroom door and lowered his voice to a whisper. "Perhaps it would be best if he did not accompany you. No attention should be called to this operation and he sometimes makes scenes."

"Leave it with me," Remo said.

Smith spoke aloud. "Give my best regards to Chiun."

"I will."

As the door closed behind Smith, the bathroom door opened. Chiun came out with two small bars of soap and a half-filled box of facial tissues. He carefully placed them into one of his trunks at the far end of the room.

Chiun slammed down the trunk lid with a crack that could have been heard even over the disco bands in the nearby town of Southampton. He picked up a small lamp and threw it through the back window of the motel room.

When he turned to Remo, his face was pale.

"Now what did he mean that I sometimes make scenes?" Chiun demanded.

The Rubout Squad had been given their first assignments by The Eraser.

Nicholas Lizzard had been told to rent two secret apartments in Bay City. He asked Sam Gregory to give him rent money in advance. Two months rent money. For two apartments.

"A thousand dollars," he said.

"That means that you're renting $250 apartments," Gregory said. "I don't think there are $250 apartments in Bay City."

"Ah, yes. Beauty must bow always before the invincible onrush of logic. Eight hundred dollars," said Lizzard who had made his mind up beforehand that he would agree to any reasonable compromise. He had figured that four hundred dollars should cover everything and anything over that was gravy. Or Vodka as the case might be.

"Here's six hundred," said Gregory, taking the money from a small leather money purse he carried in his back pocket.

"A mean and small-spirited man," mumbled Lizzard. He left the motel in Jersey City and rode into Bay City using one of the Rubout Squad's rented cars. He parked halfway down the block from Rocco Nobile's Improvement Association headquarters. He planned to get one apartment there and one apartment near the high-rise where Nobile lived.

But first a drink.

When he left the car, he took a small leather suitcase from the back seat. In the first bar he saw, he ordered, paid for and drank a Vodka. It was early in the morning and the bar was empty. He carried his suitcase into the bathroom and locked the door behind him with a hook and eye.

He opened the suitcase over the small iron-stained, scum-crusted sink. Time to go to work. But first a drink. He sipped a little Vodka from a metal flask inside the suitcase, then, almost reluctantly, capped it and put it away. Inside the suitcase was a cheap plastic makeup kit of cosmetics. Lizzard made up his eyes with false eyelashes, mascara and the dark-blue eye shadow favored by old women and prostitutes. He looked at himself. This was the part he liked best, redoing his eyes. He put on liquid makeup, to cover the blotchy broken blood vessels in his nose, then light pink lipstick and red rouge. Atop his thinning hair, he put a gray curly wig, and stepped back from the mirror. He nodded with satisfaction at his image which he thought made him look like somebody's grandmother. Quickly, he removed his sports shirt and trousers and shoes and socks and donned pantyhose, nurse-type women's shoes, and a flowered dress with a sewn-in Polyurethane bosom.

He stood in front of the mirror again, checking himself as he stuffed his male clothing into the suitcase. He was satisfied. One of his best jobs yet. That certainly called for a drink as a reward. He took a long slug out of the Vodka flask, then replaced it under his clothing and snapped the suitcase shut. Done. No one would ever know that one of America's greatest male actors hid underneath that woman's clothing and behind that painted woman's face.

He unlocked the bathroom door and peeked out. The bartender was at the end of the bar, washing glasses, his back to Lizzard, who walked quickly out the front door without looking back. He locked his suitcase in the trunk of his car.

Almost directly across the street from the Bay City Improvement Association, he found a tenement building with a for rent sign. Before ringing the super's bell, he slouched over, changing himself from a six-foot-five man to a six-foot-four woman. He rejected the idea of using a limp. It wouldn't be necessary. His disguise was already perfect. To talk to the superintendent, he used his woman's voice, a high squeaky rattle, punctuated by chuckles.

"Got a lot of apartments," the superintendent said.

"The highest one," Lizzard said. "Me and my boys, we like to be up high."

The front windows of the apartment looked down at the Nobile headquarters.

"How much, sonny?" Lizzard said.

"A hundred a month, includes heat and hot water. What's your name, Mrs.?"

"Mrs. Walker," Lizzard said. "I'll take it." He looked at the superintendent and wondered if he should come on to the burly man. He would swear the superintendent was already infatuated with Mrs. Walker from the way he was staring at "her."

"Two months in advance," the super said.

"Good," said Lizzard. He paid with two hundred in bills that had come from Sam Gregory's roll.

"Me and my boys, we'll be moving in slow over the next couple of days. We gotta wait for our furniture to come."

"Oh? Where's it coming from?"

"Chicago," Lizzard said. "But you know how movers are." He batted his false eyelashes at the superintendent who seemed very anxious to give Mrs. Walker the keys and to leave. Probably realizing that his passion was boiling almost out of control, Lizzard thought. The super went back to his first-floor apartment, where his wife asked him who had looked at the apartment.

"Some old transvestite," the super said. "Wearing women's clothes but he forgot to shave. He looks like hell."

"Pay in advance?"

"Two months."

"Good. Maybe we can attract a colony of transvestites."

Upstairs, Lizzard looked around the apartment and was satisfied with it. He decided that such a good start on the day's work entitled him to a drink or two before he went to rent the second apartment. A real drink, not some kind of hurried sip from a flask.

He was in such a hurry to get to a bar that he forgot to keep slouched over. After four vodkas, he forgot to use his woman's voice.

No one seemed to mind.

Al Baker had been directed by Sam Gregory to use all his mob contacts to find out just who was moving into Bay City, where they were moving and what they were up to.

The only problem with that assignment was that Al Baker had no mob contacts. He had run numbers in Brooklyn for five years back in the mid-Fifties, and then given it up when his brother got arrested. Since then, he had worked in a laundry, as a used car salesman, a liquor-truck driver and a drain and sewer cleaner.

He was carrying five hundred dollars of Sam Gregory's money in his pocket.

"Mafia informants don't come cheap," Baker had said. Gregory had nodded and paid.

When he had been running numbers, Baker had dreamed of working his way up through the ranks until he was the head of America's underworld. Along the way and before taking his first step up, he realized that those who reached the top didn't necessarily have to be smart. But it certainly helped if they were lucky and bullet-proof. Since he had never been lucky and he was afraid of bullets, he had lost his zeal for living the mob life. But he had never lost the fascination that came from thinking about it and talking about it, which was how he had come to Sam Gregory's attention.

Baker parked his car near River Street and wondered what to do next. "Use all your mob contacts," Gregory had said. All Al Baker knew about illegal was how to run numbers, which gave him an idea when he saw a newsstand on the corner.

Baker knew how to make people talk. To make the newsie talk, he first had to convince him that he wasn't an undercover police agent. The simplest way to do that was to badmouth politicians at every level, for cops, even undercover cops, never spoke ill of politicians who might control their destiny. The stories of what they said just might get back and they might wind up walking traffic posts in the meadows in winter.

Five minutes after going to the newsstand, Al Baker had placed a bet on a number — a small bet because he was counting on keeping most of the money Gregory had given him. He found out from the newsie that there had been a shake-up in the numbers business, that City Hall was more deeply involved now and was taking a bigger piece for protection. To stay in business, the numbers bank had had to cut the amount paid on a winning hit from 600-to-1 down to 550-to-1 and the people who bet on numbers were growling.

"Can't be much of a business anyway?" Baker said.

"Nickel and dime stuff. Every newsstand. Every candy store. Every saloon. This town so rotten, what else to do but play numbers," the newsie said. "Hope you hit it big and go to Florida 'cause this town's crap."

Baker rolled up his newspaper and began to walk away. It would do no good to spend too much time at the newsstand. Sooner or later the newsie would start asking him questions and if the cop on the numbers run saw him and didn't recognize him, he might start asking questions too. Baker waved back at the newsie.

"*You're* not going to Florida, are you?"

"Not that lucky," the newsstand owner said.

"Me neither. I'll be back tomorrow for my winnings."

As he walked away, Baker was framing the report to Gregory in his mind. "A massive infiltration of the illegal gambling industry by Rocco Nobile and his power-mad henchmen."

He walked along River Street for a while and jotted down the addresses of loft buildings which had obviously had work done on them recently or which had gotten new tenants.

In his small notebook, next to the addresses, he put a crime. He had no idea, what crimes, if any, were being perpetrated in those loft buildings so he made them up.

When he was done with his walk, his notebook read:

#358. Loansharking.

#516. Counterfeit operation.

#612. Heroin drug factory.

#764. HQ. of national auto theft ring.

He put his notebook back in his pocket. That was one side of the street. The next day, he would come back and do the other side, but first Sam Gregory would have to give him another five hundred dollars to buy off more Mafia informants.

Driving out of town, he stopped at the Bay City Bank to open a savings account. He was going to start it with $498, but he changed his mind at the last minute and only deposited $493. The other five dollars was for admission, just in case he passed a theater where *The Godfather* was playing.

Mark Tolan had also spent the day in Bay City but he was not interested in renting apartments or in who was running the numbers operation. His job was to try to clock schedules so that when The Eraser and the Rubout Squad were ready to launch their war against the Mafia, they would know what targets were vulnerable and when.

Gregory had tried to talk Tolan out of taking weapons on the mission.

"If you get picked up, it's the end of you," he had warned.

"I feel naked without a weapon," Tolan had said. "And who knows? One of those bastards may lip off to me. I want to be able to pay him back."

"We don't want random violence," Gregory said. "This is a military operation. I'm your leader. Remember the chain of command." He held up the piece of cardboard with the boxes drawn on it.

Tolan's dark eyes had blazed. "Screw the chain of command. When you're out there, alone on the streets with the beasts, you have to take care of yourself. I'm not going unarmed."

"Well, only take one gun then."

"No. I'm taking what I need. Three. The .32 caliber automatic for my jacket, the Gregory Sur-Shot for my hip and a Derringer taped to my left leg. You want me to be defenseless?"

Gregory sighed. Mark Tolan might yet prove to be difficult.

Tolan spent much of his day walking around the streets of Bay City, bumping against people as he walked, hoping against hope that one would turn and badmouth him. He crossed the street three times to try to bump into men wearing pinstripe suits, but nobody seemed to want to shoot it out in the street.

He knew that Lizzard was supposed to rent apartments to be used as sniper posts against Rocco Nobile but sniping was no fun. Tolan liked his killings up close and personal, as they had been in Nam when he had wasted everybody left behind in that VC village. He liked to see the horror on the faces. He liked to see the pain when the bullet hit home. He liked to see the movements that turned slowly to still death.

When Rocco Nobile's time came, it wouldn't be from sniping. It would be from a bullet between the eyes, fired from no more than a few steps away. By Mark Tolan.

He felt good walking along, feeling the gun on his hip and in his pocket bumping against his body. He went into the lobby of the Bay City Arms and asked about renting an apartment. He was told that all the apartments had been rented.

He was not much good at small talk so he asked the doorman, "Mayor live here?"

"Yes."

"When's he go to work?"

"Who wants to know?"

Tolan really had to draw a tight rein on himself so he didn't shoot the doorman. When he came back from Rocco Nobile, he'd pay that debt too.

He walked into City Hall and found the mayor's office on the second floor. The City Commission was meeting when he arrived and he could hear their amplified voices out in the hallway. He wondered for a moment what it would be like to jump into the room, guns blazing, and level the whole commission. That would be fun, he thought. But the real fun would come from getting the boss.

The mayor's receptionist was a pretty young brunette named Denise. He asked her how to go about getting an appointment with the mayor. He was told to write a letter or he could leave a telephone number and she would get back to him. Of course, she'd have to know what the meeting concerned.

"Mayor here every day?" he asked.

"Every day."

"I'll spell everything out in my letter." Before leaving he glanced to his left. Through a leaded glass window, he could see another secretary at a desk. Sitting in a chair, leaning against the wall, was a man reading a paper. The man looked like a bodyguard.

Tolan thought how easy it would be. One shot in the head on this young twit, Denise. Push through the door. Two more bullets to take care of the other secretary and the bodyguard. He would not even have to break stride. He could be in the mayor's office before the mayor would have a chance to react. He could put a bullet in the ginzo's brain before anybody could do anything.

He reached under his jacket to feel the cold butt of the gun on his right hip. Then he withdrew his hand, slowly, reluctantly. He didn't want it to be a surprise shot. He wanted Nobile to know he was in danger, that there was a killer after him, and when the time came, he wanted to see Nobile squirm a little bit before he finished him off. It was the fright on their faces that he really liked.

As he left City Hall, he hoped to himself that Rocco Nobile had friends. Gregory had said that they were going to live huge, but all he wanted to do was to kill huge.

It was going to be fun and it was going to be easy. And anybody who got in his way was going to be hurt. Terminally.

Yeah, he thought. Yeah.

CHAPTER EIGHT

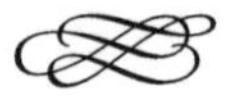

THE PING PONG BALL WHIZZED off Chiun's fingertips. It headed straight across the room toward Remo's left hand. At the last split second, the ball veered upward and sharply to the right, toward Remo's head. Before it touched flesh, Remo drove his right hand forward. The hard fingertips slammed into the center of the ball. The little plastic sphere broke in two halves, which rapped off the panelled wall of the motel room with an almost simultaneous *tap-tap* sound. The rug near the wall was littered with half ping pong balls.

"I don't like this assignment, Little Father," Remo said.

"Why not?" Chiun asked. He was reaching toward a box of ping pong balls on the table behind him.

"Because we're bodyguards again. I don't like being a bodyguard. That's not what you trained me for."

"I like you as a bodyguard better than I like you as a detective," Chiun said. "For that, you are totally untrained." He flashed another ping pong ball at Remo from behind his back. The ball arced toward the younger man in a high lazy loop, then at the last moment, seemed to increase in speed. Remo got his left hand up to block the ball from hitting his face, but his stroke was not perfect, and instead of the fingertips splitting the ball in two, they merely dented it and drove it hard off the wood-panelled wall.

"Don't carp about my being a detective," Remo said.

"I never carp," Chiun said. "You should not mind being called a bodyguard. To be a bodyguard in time of trouble means that we will practice our assassin's art. And, if it is not a time of trouble, who cares what we are called because we are paid for resting?"

"Maybe you're right," Remo said.

Chiun put his hands at his sides, signaling that the exercise had entered a rest period. Remo relaxed.

"You must remember," Chiun said, "that Emperor Smith is crazy just as all emperors are crazy. They never know what we do. But he always pays on time. You buy what you wish. The gold gets to the village of Sinanju on time." He paused. "Did I ever tell you why that is important?"

"Yes, Chiun," Remo said wearily. "No more than five hundred times though. Poor village, throw babies into bay to drown when there's not enough to eat, masters work as assassins for emperors, get money, feed village, no more drowning kids. I got it. See, I know it well."

"It does not always work thusly," Chiun said "Once, with the Master Shang-tu-

"Never heard of him," Remo said. He had heard of the Eng and Chiun and Wo-Ti and a half dozen other Masters down through history, including the greatest of them all, the great Master Wang, but Chiun's lecturing had, up till now, never mentioned Shang-tu.

"He was not memorable," Chiun said. "He produced no new art and he produced no new business. He was content merely to service accounts that Masters before him had created. One of these accounts was a Siamese king, for whom Shang-tu had performed a great service. Yet, Shang-tu did not do the most important thing an assassin must do."

"What's that?" asked Remo.

"He did not secure the payment. He accepted instead the king's promise that the payment would be sent to Sinanju, but when Shang-tu returned, the payment had not come, and after many months, it still had not come and the villagers were starving and it was time to send the children home again into the bay, because there was no food for them to eat."

Remo watched Chiun. Under the guise of talking to Remo and explaining this story, the old Korean's hand was slipping quietly behind him, toward the box of ping pong balls.

"What happened?" asked Remo, watching without appearing to watch.

Chiun's hand dropped back to his side, away from the box.

"Shang-tu had to go back to see the king once more and the king made profuse apologies and blamed the failure to pay on one of his ministers and in the presence of the Master, he had the minister executed. And he told the Master to go home because now, surely, the payment would be there at Sinanju. And Shang-tu went back to Sinanju, but the payment did not come, and now many children had been sent home to the sea and the people of the village raised their voice against Shang-tu." Chiun's right hand was again moving toward the box of ping pong balls. Remo slightly tensed his body. Chiun's hand moved away again.

"So Shang-tu went back to Siam again," Remo said.

Chiun looked up sharply. "That is correct. Did I ever tell you this story before?"

"No."

"Then please do not interrupt. So the Master Shang-tu went back to Siam again. This time, with the blood of many children on his head, he did not listen to the king's honeyed words, but instead he slew the king and carried back the treasure himself. And that is an important lesson for all assassins and we are indebted to Shang-tu for teaching it to us. Hail Shang-tu."

"Don't trust anybody, even kings," Remo suggested.

Chiun shook his head. "Don't you ever listen?"

"I listened. I listened. It sounded like don't trust anybody."

"Really, Remo, you're hopeless." He raised his hands to show how hopeless Remo was. He moved a few inches to the left so that his body was directly in front of the box of ping pong balls. When he lowered his hands, he slid them behind him so that either hand could reach the box.

"Trust anyone you want, but make sure you get paid," Chiun said.

"That's the lesson?" Remo asked. He tensed his body again. He didn't know which hand the ping pong ball would come at him from. He divided his balance between both feet so he could move easily in either direction.

Chiun's hands were moving behind his back as he spoke.

"Of course," he said. "Nothing is more important to an assassin. And although Emperor Smith is a lunatic, he pays on time. If his wishes are for you to call yourself a bodyguard, call yourself a bodyguard." He winked and Remo knew the ping pong assault was only a split second away. "The inventive assassin can always find a way to turn any job into his own special art, and emperors never know the difference."

Suddenly, both Chiun's hands came out from behind his kimono. Remo lowered himself into an at-ready crouch. His hands came up toward his face. Chiun's hands moved at a blur. They lifted toward Remo, then opened. Remo peered intently for the flash of the ping pong ball. But there was no ball. Chiun's hands dropped to his sides.

He smiled again. "Sometimes the threat of an attack is more powerful than the attack itself," he said. "A ping pong ball would not hurt you. But you could be killed by being off balance and tense."

"I liked my explanation of the legend better," Remo said. "You can't trust anybody."

He turned away from Chiun. As he did, he was hit in the back of the head with a ping pong ball. It rebounded off his skull against the wall with a hard piercing rap.

"If you trust no one," Chiun said, "then you never have reason to be surprised."

Remo sighed. "Let's go see Rocco Nobile and start being bodyguards."

As they left their room and walked toward the rented white Lincoln Continental, a burly, dark-haired man with muscular sloping shoulders bulging through his Qiana shirt stepped from a room two doors away from theirs.

He called to Remo.

"Hey, you."

Remo looked at the man. His eyes were dark and his lips were fish-thin. He had big hands which he had clenched tightly at his side. A man under tension, Remo thought.

"You mean me?" Remo asked.

"Yeah, you. You finally finished with that ping pong game?"

"Ping pong? Ping pong?" Remo said. He remembered the exercise. The sound of the balls hitting the wall. "Yeah, we're all done," he said.

"Good thing," the man said.

"Why?"

"Because if you didn't stop, I was coming over to shove those paddles up your ass."

"It's harder to hit the ball that way," Remo said.

"Oh, yeah?"

"Sure. Think about it," Remo said. "You do think, don't you?"

"You're a wise guy, aren't you?" the big man said.

Remo looked into the car at Chiun. Chiun shrugged and Remo thought of Rocco Nobile and said mildly, "Some other time, pal. Some other time."

"Any time," the big man said. He brought his two ham fists together and began cracking his knuckles.

"I won't forget," Remo said as he got into the car, closed the door and drove from the motel lot.

Mark Tolan watched the car go. Ping pong. What kind of faggots played ping pong in the daytime in a motel room? For exercise? Yeah, he'd give them exercise. Yeah. He went back inside his own room where Sam Gregory sat at the window table, drawing maps and charts and tables of organization and plans.

Al Baker was sprawled on the bed watching a television game show whose major premise seemed to be that terminal retardation could be fun. Its minor premise was that all the people on the show were terminally retarded and its conclusion, therefore, was that the show was fun. Al Baker never missed it. He watched three young men, hiding behind a screen, trying to be glib and clever as they were asked questions by a young woman who couldn't see them. Baker fantasized being on the show, sitting on one of the high stools.

"And if we went out together, Number Three, what would we probably do?"

"I'd give you a beef injection, lady," Baker saw himself saying.

The girl squealed, *"Ooooooh."*

"When I'm done with you, you'll be halfway into the cracks on the floor."

At this time in his fantasy, the girl always gasped, *"Quick, get rid of the others. I want Number Three. And I want him now."* Then she fainted.

Baker never missed a game show. He pictured himself on all of them, writing new scripts, always winning women and money.

"You still watching that crap?"

Baker looked toward the door, where Mark Tolan hulked menacingly.

"Yeah. What's it to you?"

"I hate that show," Tolan said.

His face was twisted into a death's head snarl. He frightened Baker. Tolan was obviously a homicidal maniac and Baker couldn't understand why Sam Gregory had recruited this ding-a-ling.

"I like it," Baker said. Tolan's face twisted some more.

"I'll change it if you want," Baker said. "It's almost over anyway."

"Is there a war movie on?"

"No."

"Then watch anything you want, creep. Maybe you'll get smart if you watch enough shows."

"Will you two stop bickering?" Gregory said, looking up from the table.

"When are we gonna start doing something except sitting around here, listening to some faggots play ping pong next door and watching you draw maps?" Tolan demanded.

"We're waiting for The Lizzard to return," Gregory said. He had taken to calling Nicholas Lizzard "The Lizzard." He thought it gave the operation more of a touch of glamor. He called Al Baker "The Baker." He wanted to give Mark Tolan a name too. It wasn't that he couldn't think of one. He had a lot of them in mind. The Mutilator. The Extincter. The Avenger. It was just that he was afraid any one of them might rub Tolan the wrong way and he might wind up wasting everybody on the team. It wouldn't do for the members of the Rubout Squad to be rubbed out by one of their own. Especially The Eraser, Sam Gregory himself. He had to live. Bay City was just the first. He was going to go on, across the country, town after town, city after city, tracking the mob down in its lair, wherever he found them. They would learn to fear The Eraser.

"What the hell do we need Gizzard for?" Tolan said. "He's as worthless as tits on a bull. Let's get going. Let's go kill somebody."

"Tomorrow," Gregory said quickly. "I'm working up the plans now."

"We going after Nobile?"

"Not yet. First we're going to hit one of those mob businesses that The Baker infiltrated today."

"He couldn't infiltrate a phone booth with a dime," Tolan said, sneering over at Baker who was envisioning himself lying on the beach at Waikiki with the girl from the game show.

Baker didn't answer. He was wondering if the $493 he had in the bank would get him to Hawaii.

Gregory said, "The Baker has found a drug factory on River Street. We're going to hit it tomorrow."

"Good," said Tolan. He turned toward the motel room window and pointed his finger at passing cars, squeezing an imaginary trigger and going "Bang, bang" softly under his breath. He could imagine the first shot hitting into a driver's temple, killing him instantly. The second shot took out the right front tire, throwing the car out of control, across the center divider into the oncoming lane. Cars piled up by the dozens. Bodies littered the streets. Some cars caught fire. A few exploded. Burning gasoline flew into the air and droplets fell on passersby with flammable clothes. A baby carriage burned.

Tolan smiled.

"How come I don't have no name?" he asked the window.

Gregory said, "What do you mean?" He knew very well what Tolan meant.

"You're The Eraser. You call that creep The Baker. You call the drunk The Lizzard. What are you going to call me?"

"You mean to your face?" Baker called out.

"Funny," Tolan said grimly.

"How about The Lunatic?" Baker suggested.

Tolan wheeled around. His eyes blazed hatred. Baker tried to bury himself deeper into the mattress.

"That ain't funny," Tolan said. "I'd like to put you away, television man."

Baker coughed. "Don't try it, buddy. I've got a lot of connected friends. They'd be on you like a coat of paint."

"You ain't connected to your ass," Tolan said.

"No? You'll see," Baker said.

"Send 'em on," said Tolan. "Send 'em all on. I want them all. All your ginzo friends."

"Stop it, you two," Gregory said. He met Tolan's eyes and tried not to shudder. "What name would you like?" he asked.

Tolan thought for a moment. Yeah, he thought. He wanted a name. Yeah. Some thing that would strike terror into the hearts of the bugs of the Mafia. They were all bugs, yeah. Bugs. "Bugs," he said softly.

"Sounds good to me," Baker said. "'Bugs.'"

"Shut up," Tolan said. Yeah, they were bugs and he was the man who was going to take care of all of them. Live huge. Yeah, he would live huge, and kill bugs. "The Exterminator," he said.

He looked at Gregory and a small smile creased the lines around his mouth.

"Yeah, that's it. The Exterminator."

"All right. The Exterminator it is," Gregory said.

"I liked Bugs better," said Baker.

"When we're done here," Tolan said, "you and I are going to have it out." He looked at Baker who waved a hand at him in disregard. Baker wasn't that worried. He had it figured out. He had never killed anyone in his life and, if truth be told, he could never remember throwing a punch at anybody in anger. But this time, it would be different. Tolan was going to get him when they were done? Well, exactly ten minutes before they were done in Bay City, Baker was going to put a bullet in the back of Tolan's head. Nobody could fault him for that.

Gregory spoke again. "The Eraser and his Rubout Squad: The Exterminator, The Baker and The Lizzard. Sounds good to me. And tomorrow we're going to hit this drug factory. I've got the plans worked out now. We're going to pick away at all the goons in this city and then we're going to get Rocco Nobile." He paused. "It's time for another note."

He looked around and found a yellow pad but couldn't find another pencil. "I need more pencils," he said.

Tolan was still staring out the window, pointing his finger at passing cars. "I'll get 'em. Any special kind?"

"The ones that write," Baker said.

"Yellow wooden ones," Gregory said quickly. "With an eraser. If you can get Eberhard Faber Mongols, get them. You got money?"

Baker heard money mentioned and sat up in bed. "I'll go," he volunteered.

"I'm going," Tolan said. "And I've got what I need." He walked from the room.

While he was gone, The Lizzard returned to the room. Or was returned. He was spilled out of a taxicab by the driver. His gray wig was on sideways and he could barely stand. Walking was out of the question.

Gregory saw him through the window and called, "Baker. Go get The Lizzard. He seems to be having some trouble."

Baker went outside. The Lizzard recognized him and smiled. He batted his remaining single false eyelash.

"Hiya big boy," he said thickly, in a high-pitched squawk. He winked. "Wanna get it on?"

"Oh, shut up," Baker said. "You're slammed up again." He threw an arm around The Lizzard's back and helped him toward the door.

"'S'not true. Not drunk," said Lizzard.

"Bullshit," said Baker.

Inside the room, Gregory said, "You're drunk."

"Just a pose," Lizzard said. "So no one recognize me." His wig now had slipped so far down on his face that it covered his eyes. He kept swatting at it and missing.

"Did you get the apartments?" Gregory demanded.

"Got one. Sherioush houshing shortage in Bay City. Had to look very hard. Got good leadsh for tomorrow. Men want to buy me drinksh all the time."

"Put him in bed," Gregory said.

Baker pushed Lizzard toward the bed. He fell like a solitary tree, hacked down in the middle of an open field. He was asleep before he landed.

"When he sobers up," Gregory said. "We'll find out where the apartment is. We may need it tomorrow when we make our daring daylight raid on that drug headquarters."

Baker nodded. He wished he could remember what address he had said housed the drug operation. Maybe he could get some more money tonight from Gregory for a pre-attack reconnaissance operation.

CHAPTER NINE

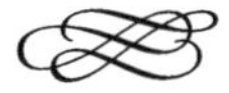

"TELL HIM REMO IS HERE," Remo told Denise, the receptionist in the mayor's outer office.

"Yes sir," the young woman said. She smiled at Remo. "You want to stand here alongside me while I telephone him?" She motioned to a spot behind the desk, next to her right side.

"Sure," said Remo.

"Where will I stand?" Chiun asked the young woman. "I am here too."

"I thought you might prefer to sit, sir," Denise said.

"No. I want to hear too," Chiun said. "I will stand there." He pointed to her left side and came over to stand alongside her.

The pretty woman dialed three digits. "A Mr. Remo is here to see you, sir."

She nodded.

"Yes, sir." She replaced the telephone. She smiled up at Remo as she said, "You may go right in."

"Thank you." Remo turned away and the girl grabbed his left hand. "Wait," she said. "I'll show you in." She stood up. "When you're done, would you like a tour of City Hall?"

"I don't think so," Remo said.

"I have time. It's almost my lunch hour," she said.

"It's three o'clock," Remo said.

"I take late lunches. Really. Honest. I could show you around. It'd be no trouble at all."

She pressed her chest against Remo.

"No trouble at all," she said.

"He does not want to go," Chiun said. "That should be obvious to you. But ask me. Perhaps I will take this wonderful tour."

"Yes, sir," the girl said unhappily. "This way, please."

She ushered them past the mayor's personal secretary and a man who sat outside the door, with his arms folded, leaning back in his chair against the wall. He looked at Remo and sneered as Remo walked by. Remo stuck out his tongue and crossed his eyes. The man's hand moved toward his right pocket. Chiun brushed against the man and his fingertips touched the man's right bicep. The man's right arm stopped moving toward his pocket, frozen in position as if it had just been sprayed with liquid hydrogen.

He looked at Chiun in surprise, then at his arm. He gritted his teeth as he tried to move his arm, but he could not. He grabbed his right wrist with his left hand and tried to force his arm down but it would not move. His eyes glittered with panic and he tried to calm himself because he had heard that if you stay still after having a stroke, your chances of survival are better.

The receptionist showed Remo and Chiun into the mayor's office. They stood inside the door and waited for the heavy oaken door to close behind her.

"I'm Remo."

Rocco Nobile put a finger to his lips in a *shush*ing gesture. He reached behind him to a large walnut AM-FM radio and turned it to a rock station. He turned the volume up loud.

"Lock the door," he told Remo.

Remo locked the door and Nobile motioned them forward to his desk, and rose to come around to talk to them.

"The radio's in case anybody's got this office bugged. It messes them up. Glad to meet you, Remo."

"I am Chiun."

"And you, Chiun."

"You've been expecting us," Remo said.

"Right. I was told you'd be coming. You know what's going down here?"

Remo was surprised to hear the voice of Wardell Pinkerton the Third come out of the face and body of Rocco Nobile. The mayor looked like the head-waiter in a Greek restaurant but the voice that came out was Ivy League and soft.

"Yeah, we know," Remo said. "We were told to keep you alive."

"By whom?" asked Nobile.

"By Emperor- Chiun began. Remo interrupted him. "It's probably best, Mayor, if you don't know that."

Nobile nodded. "All right. What do you think?"

"I think we've got to stay as close to you as the smell of garlic," Remo said.

"I might have trouble with my other bodyguards," Nobile said.

"Was that one outside the door?" Chiun asked. Nobile nodded.

"You will have no trouble with him," Chiun said. "He is very worried about his arm."

"Where's the other one?" Remo asked.

"He stays at the apartment to make sure nobody plants anything."

"He can keep doing that for a while," Remo said. "Just give us a cover story. Nobody has to know who we are."

"All right. I'll make you- Nobile hesitated as he thought. "You can be from the West Coast, checking out the place before your bosses move any operations here. And Mr. Chiun can be a Chinese connection for cocaine."

"Good," said Remo.

"Not good," said Chiun. "That will never do."

"Why not?' Remo asked.

"I am not Chinese. I am Korean. Do I look Chinese? Would such a story fool anyone? Do I look Chinese?" He looked toward Mayor Nobile for an answer.

"Say no," Remo advised.

"No," said Nobile. "All right. We'll make you a Korean connection for cocaine."

"North Korean," said Chiun.

"North Korean," amended Nobile.

"Good," said Chiun. "Now that we have the important business out of the way, all that is left are mere details."

CHAPTER TEN

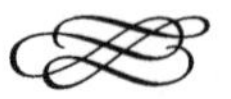

FROM THEIR CAR ACROSS THE STREET, The Eraser and the Rubout Squad looked at the old loft building on River Street. The Lizzard had left his men's clothing in the trunk of the car yesterday and he could not remember where he had parked the car, so he was still wearing the flowered dress, the gray wig and his makeup from the previous day. His whiskered stubble had grown an extra day longer. He had powdered it to make it lighter.

"This is it?" asked Gregory.

"Absolutely," said Al Baker. He had no idea what the place was. He had conned Gregory out of two hundred dollars the night before to do a little more infiltration work, but when he had gotten to the loft building, it was closed for the night. So when he got back to the motel, he had no choice but to tell Gregory that absolutely and positively, the building housed a major drug operation. Maybe it did. Who knew? Who else would move into Bay City except somebody doing something illegal?

"A big narcotics factory, right?" Gregory said again.

"No doubt about it," Baker said. "That's what my sources in the Family tell me."

"All right. This is what we do. Lizzard, you go upstairs and case the joint. Find out what they're doing and who's up there. Then come down and tell us and we'll move. We want to be sure it's not a trap."

"Who'd set a trap for us?" Tolan said. "Nobody knows we're even alive, Gregory."

"You can't be too sure, Exterminator," said Gregory. "And please call me Eraser."

Fearful of an ambush, terrified of being killed, Nicholas Lizzard walked across the street and through the ground floor door of the factory building. He looked back toward the car for encouragement and Sam Gregory waved him on.

Upstairs, Lizzard found a small hall sign that read: *Wo Fat Fortune Cookie Company.*

While he waited in the hallway, looking around and listening, inside the second floor factory, Mr. and Mrs. Wo Fat and their three children were busy preparing the ingredients for the day's batch of fortune cookies. They were still congratulating themselves on their good fortune. When their factory had been gutted by fire the previous week, none of their heavy bakery machinery had been damaged and they were able to move right into this new loft a block away. They had lost only three days of work in both the fire and the move.

Lizzard pushed open the door and stepped inside. Mr. and Mrs. Wo Fat looked at him and he remembered to hunch over to hide his six-foot-five frame and, smiling winsomely, he walked to a counter just inside the door.

Wo Fat, an oily looking man with white powder on his pudgy hands, came to the counter.

"Yes, Ma'am, I help you?"

"I want to buy some fortune cookies."

"Yes, Ma'am. How many?"

"There are four of us," said The Lizzard.

He looked around. The place looked normal enough but Orientals were devious. Who knew what they were up to? Mrs. Wo Fat walked through a back door into the kitchen area in the back of the loft. Through the open door, on a big butcher block table, The Lizzard saw a large mound of white powder. Heroin. He knew it. Baker had been right. The Lizzard was pretty sure that heroin was white. It was always white on television.

"I get for you," Wo Fat said.

The Oriental walked into the kitchen and chuckled to his wife as she helped their three children measure out the mound of white flour on the table into small stainless steel mixing bowls.

In Chinese, he said, "Strange person. Want four fortune cookies."

"Be careful," his wife said. "That look like woman but is man. Hands too big and bony for woman."

Wo Fat nodded and took four freshly-baked fortune cookies from a tray next to the large ovens. He put them in a small brown bag and went back to the counter. But the old woman was not there. She had gone.

Wo Fat shrugged, opened the bag and bit into one of the cookies himself. He smiled, as he always did when eating his own wares. The cookies were good. Thirty years in the business and his were the best. He knew it and was proud of it.

He leaned with his back on the counter and through the open door to the spotless kitchen watched his wife and their children at work. His was the smile of the talented craftsman.

In the hallway, The Lizzard pointed to the door.

"That's it."

"Everybody ready?" Gregory asked. He looked around. Mark Tolan had a gun in each hand. In his right hand, he held the Gregory Sur-Shot. In his left, he clutched a .357 Magnum. Al Baker held a .32 caliber revolver delicately by the butt end as if he were afraid it was going to give him a shock. The Lizzard had no gun. Gregory handed him a .45 automatic. The Lizzard didn't want it. He pushed it away. Gregory slapped it into his open hand.

Gregory himself held another Sur-Shot.

"All right," he hissed. "Ready…get set-

Before he got to go, Mark Tolan had kicked his way through the unlocked door into the fortune cookie factory. Wo Fat turned at the noise and caught a fragmenting bullet in the middle of his forehead. He slumped behind the counter, his hand dragging the bag of fortune cookies onto the floor.

Through the door to the kitchen, Tolan saw the mound of white powder and realized that was the cutting room where the heroin was mixed with powdered sugar into a smaller, weaker dosage for sale on the streets.

He raced toward the door. Behind him, Gregory, Baker and Lizzard came into the loft. When Lizzard saw Wo Fat's body with his head blown away, he vomited on the floor. Baker put his gun in his pocket, determined not to use it under any circumstances, except to shoot Tolan. They followed Gregory back toward the kitchen where Tolan had entered.

The Exterminator had met the rest of Wo Fat's family coming toward the door to investigate the sound of the first shot.

"Yellow peril," he screamed. "Angels of the Mafia devil. Die!" Firing with both hands, he cut down Mrs. Wo Fat and then their three young children. When the four bodies lay motionless on the floor, Tolan looked down at them, smiling the satisfied smile of the redeemed avenger. He saw the white powder on their hands and for good measure, emptied his guns into their dead bodies.

The three other men joined him.

"Oh, God," said Lizzard, wiping the retch from his mouth.

"Looney," said Baker. "Frigging looney."

Gregory was silent. Tolan pointed toward the pile of powder. "There it is. The heroin," he said. He looked-around. "Got to set this place afire," he said. "Destroy that heroin so no one else gets it."

He saw several jars of cooking alcohol and sprinkled it over a pile of paper boxes in the corner. He lit it with a match and the boxes flared and the fire almost instantly began spreading to the old dry wooden walls.

"It'll go in a flash. Better get out of here," Gregory said.

Behind him, Al Baker touched a finger to the pile of white powder and placed it in his mouth. Just as he had feared. It was flour, used to make fortune cookies. He had been wrong. He felt sick.

He had no chance to mention it because the other men were running back toward the front door.

Suddenly Tolan stopped.

"Forgot something," he said. He reached into the back pocket of his pants and took out a handful of yellow pencils which he had taken from the box he had obtained for Gregory the day before.

He snapped a half dozen of them in his hands and threw the eraser ends at the Chinese bodies in the kitchen doorway.

"There," he said happily. "Let them know The Eraser and the Rubout Squad were here. And The Exterminator."

Then he followed the other three men down the steps. They ran across the street and fled in their rented car.

The mayor's regular driver was still in the hospital having tests made to determine the extent of nerve injury suffered in his right arm, so Remo was driving the limousine. Chiun and Rocco Nobile were in the back seat. Remo had given Chiun strict orders, which he had couched as a humble request from the Emperor to the all-knowing, all-noble personage of the Master of Sinanju that Chiun not tell Rocco Nobile anything about CURE or Harold W. Smith or secret organizations. Without knowing it, Rocco Nobile had been working for CURE for almost five years and if he had gone that long in the dark, it was probably best to keep him there. Remo knew that Smith wanted to be sure that, in case Rocco Nobile's cover was ever blown, the man would be in no position to drop anything dangerous about CURE.

Remo had explained all this to Chiun. Chiun had agreed that he would not utter a word to Rocco Nobile.

Now as Remo drove, he heard Chiun in the back seat say to Nobile:

"I know something you don't know."

"Chiun," Remo said.

The car radio crackled on.

"Fire in progress at 612 River Street."

"Let's go over there," Nobile said.

"You like fires?" Remo said, glad to change the subject from what Chiun knew that Rocco Nobile didn't.

"Not really," Nobile said, "but I guess the mayor ought to be around for one."

They parked in the street behind a fire engine. Flames were spitting from the second floor window of the old loft building. Firemen were standing on the street pouring water into the building. Another crew was on top of a cherry picker, fifty feet in the air, pumping water down onto the roof of the low building, and also spraying adjoining buildings to try to stop the fire from spreading to the other old wood structures.

Remo and Chiun followed Nobile up to a fire officer wearing a white helmet with a gold medallion on the front.

"Anybody in there, Chief?" Nobile asked.

"We don't know. We can't get in yet."

Chiun looked at Remo and Remo nodded. The two men drifted away from the mayor and the chief who stood staring up at the building. Licks of flame began to spit through the roof. The two men moved around the crews of firemen and then darted toward the ground level doorway.

"Hey, you can't- one firemen shouted. But Remo and Chiun were already inside. He turned to the man next to him.

"Two guys went in that building."

"Whaaaa?"

"Two guys went in. You didn't see them?"

"No. I didn't see nothing. You sure?"

"Sure, I'm sure," the fireman said. He thought for a moment of what he had seen. A skinny white man with a black T-shirt and black trousers. A tiny old Oriental wearing a gold brocade kimono.

A gold brocade kimono? At 9 A.M.? In Bay City?

He shook his head. Not likely.

"I think maybe the smoke's gotten to me. I'm getting some oxygen," he said and walked back toward the emergency wagon where oxygen demand tanks with masks were propped up against the rear tire.

Remo and Chiun slid through flame up the sway-backed wooden steps toward the second floor.

"In there," Chiun said, pointing toward Wo Fat's factory. "It started there."

As Remo opened the door, a *whoosh* of hot air and flames flared out at their faces. After the first surge had subsided, they moved inside and Chiun closed the door behind them to seal off the draft. The entire second floor was ablaze. Flames burned up off the wooden floor. The old wooden walls were on fire and tongues of flame poured through the doorway of the kitchen area in the back.

Remo ran toward the kitchen, but as he passed the counter, he saw Wo Fat's body, so far untouched by flames. On its chest, he saw the broken half of a pencil and picked it up.

Inside the kitchen door, they found the partially burned bodies of Wo Fat's wife and three children. The two men saw where the slugs had bitten into their bodies. Flames chewed around them like some giant insidious dragon tongue.

Remo saw several charred pieces of wood lying near the bodies. He picked them up and stuck them in his shirt pocket.

"We should get these bodies out of here," he hissed at Chiun.

The old man shook his head.

"No. Let them be victims of the fire."

Remo thought for a split second and realized Chiun was right. Five members of a family killed in a fire was a tragedy, but five people shot to death might just blow everything CURE and Smith and Nobile were trying to do in Bay City.

The fire was crackling in the ceiling over their heads and Chiun looked up. Through the wood panels, he could see a sliver of blue sky.

"We best go," he said. He pointed to the roof.

As Remo looked up, the first of the beams burned through and a large panel of roof ripped loose with a wrenching tear and came down at them, pouring plaster and wood and tons of water at them. The two men darted back as the massive pile hit near their feet, shuddering the fire-weakened floor and causing it to creak ominously and tilt.

"Whole building's going, Chiun," Remo said. "Let's go."

They ran back past Wo Fat's body, through the flames that surrounded the door and down the wooden stairs. This time they left the upstairs door open behind them and the flames *whooshed* out into the hallway as if the door to a huge coal-burning furnace had suddenly been opened in a gas-filled room.

They paused at the bottom of the steps and then slipped out into a mix of firemen milling around the entrance. The fireman who thought he had seen two men enter the building was just coming off the oxygen mask. He looked up. Behind the cluster of firefighters, he saw the two men again. The thin white one. The old Oriental with the golden kimono. He gulped and went back for more oxygen.

In the back seat of the limousine, Remo showed Rocco Nobile the pieces of wood he had picked up in the building.

"Five bodies," he said. "We left them there."

Nobile looked at him as if to question why, then nodded. He understood.

He fingered the pieces of wood. They were tops of pencils.

"The Eraser," Nobile said.

Remo nodded.

"That was a fortune cookie factory run by a Chinese family," Nobile said. "Why would this Eraser hit there?"

"I don't know. Maybe he thought they were somebody else. You got any cops in this town?

"Of course."

"Real cops?"

"I don't know. I think so. Why?"

"You can read the name on one of these pencil tops. Why don't you send some cops around quietly and find out if anybody bought a box of them in any stores around here?"

"I'll get them on it right away," Nobile said.

Remo drove the mayor and Chiun back to City Hall. The mail was already on Nobile's desk. On top of it was an unstamped envelope with a bulge in it. When Nobile saw it, his stomach sank.

He pointed at it to Remo, who opened the letter.

The broken top of a pencil fell onto the desk. The note was hand printed:

THOSE HEROIN PUSHERS WERE JUST THE FIRST. WE ARE COMING FOR YOU, NOBILE.

THE ERASER.

"I don't understand," Nobile said. "They just made fortune cookies. What heroin?"

Remo was in the doorway talking to the secretary.

"Where'd this letter come from?"

"Somebody gave it to Denise."

Remo talked to Denise, who was happy to talk to Remo. And Denise had a good eye. The envelope was dropped off by a man in drag. "A big tall skinny thing, but he was wearing a wig and woman's clothes. But it was a man."

"Thanks, honey," Remo said. "I owe you."

"When do I collect?" Denise said.

CHAPTER ELEVEN

The New York Times didn't carry it. The *New York Post* didn't carry it. Some of the Jersey papers gave it a couple of paragraphs, and of all the New York newspapers, only the *Daily News* carried it.

Their item read:

Bad Fortune

Five members of a Chinese family were burned to death in Bay City yesterday when the family fortune cookie factory, located in a loft building near the city's decaying waterfront, was gutted by flames.

The Eraser read the item and saw instantly that the evil hand of the Mafia had also infiltrated the New York press. Why else would they cover up a story that should have read:

Eraser and Rubout Squad Declare War on Mafia

Five members of an international heroin ring were gunned down yesterday in their secret drug factory in Bay City, New Jersey.

Near their bodies, police found a hundred million billion zillion dollars in uncut heroin. Also found in the building, as a warning to evil-doers, were the eraser ends of a half dozen pencils. This is the trademark of The Eraser and his Rubout Squad, who have vowed to wipe organized crime from the face of Bay City, as their first step toward cleansing America of this insidious evil.

Sam Gregory thought he would give them just one more chance, as he tossed the newspapers to the floor of his motel room.

He called the City Desk of *The New York Times* first.

"Hello, City Desk."

"This is The Eraser. My Rubout Squad and I killed those five people in Bay City yesterday. This is just the first skirmish in our war to the death against the Mafia."

Following the *Times'* normal policy for dealing with madmen on the telephone, the copy boy said, "Why don't you write us a letter about it?" before hanging up.

The *Daily News* was kinder. The man on the City Desk patiently explained that they had already done a story on the tragedy in Bay City.

"But you called it a fire," Gregory protested.

"The building burned down. Generally, that indicates a fire," the man said.

"Yeah, but we set it to destroy the heroin. After we got rid of those drug dealers who are poisoning America's bodies and minds."

"Hang on a moment. There was a two-minute wait and the man came back to the telephone. "By dirty drug dealers, you mean Suzie Wo Fat, 13, Tommy Wo Fat, 14, and Eddie Wo Fat, 11?"

"They were all part of it," Gregory said.

"Go fuck yourself."

Only the *New York Post* was interested, in keeping with the paper's long-term policy of being interested in everything a day late.

The city editor gave the assignment to a twenty-three-year-old reporter who had finished first in his class at college, majoring in Cultural Anthropology, Aspects of Abnormality in the White Mind, Social Repression in America, and Making Revolutions Work, and had convinced the publisher that all these were good substitutes for the ability to write a simple declarative English sentence.

Remo was in Rocco Nobile's office when the *Post* reporter's call came through.

"Mayor Nobile? This is Peter Plennary of the *Post.*"

Nobile nodded to Remo and pressed a button which turned the telephone into a loudspeaker so Remo could listen in.

"Yes, this is Mayor Nobile."

"We received a telephone call from someone claiming to be responsible for the fire yesterday. The fortune-cookie fire?"

"I see. Did he say who he was?"

"He said he was The Eraser and that those Chinese were in the heroin trade and he was declaring war against the Mafia, and I want to know why you're protecting the Mafia, because I know all about you New Jersey politicians, working over here in New York."

"Isn't that awful?" Mayor Nobile said.

"What's awful? What do you mean?" the reporter asked suspiciously.

"It's awful how tragedies like this have a way of bringing out the bedbugs."

"He said he shot the members of that family."

"Well, that should prove to you that the poor man was deranged. That family died in the fire. There were no gunshot wounds."

"Oh, I see."

"And just for your information, the Wo Fat family had lived in Bay City for thirty years. They had operated that bakery all that time. They were never arrested for anything."

"Oh, I see," said the reporter.

"Anything else?" Nobile asked.

"No, I guess not," Peter Plennary said.

"I hope you're not going to run a story on this," Nobile said.

"Why not?"

"Because these things have a ripple effect. One lunatic gets some publicity out of a tragedy and it encourages him to really try to create a tragedy. Or imitators try to do the same. It would be awful if some poor demented person actually did start a fire to kill someone."

"I see," the reporter said.

"Did this Eraser person say who he was?"

"No. Why?"

"I just wanted to let my police know so they could keep alert for demented persons who might fit his description."

"Oh, I see," said Peter Plennary, but he did not see at all. He just couldn't understand why anybody would want to call in the fascist police establishment to deal with an arson case. If Rocco Nobile wasn't a fascist, he would have asked the fire department to watch out for the suspected fire-setter. Anyone knew that.

When Peter Plennary hung up, he was convinced he was on to something. He had a big story. A Mafia mayor and that was obvious because he had an Italian name. Some wonderful person risking his own life to try to fight the Mafia. A gang of Chinese heroin-peddlers. The children probably were not children at all but cleverly disguised midgets. It could be a really exciting story. Peter Plennary started work on it right away. He wrote two hundred and fourteen pages. When he turned it in seven weeks later, his editor had forgotten what it was about and threw it in the garbage. Plennary retrieved it late at night when the editor had gone home and decided to use it as his doctoral thesis: "Crime and Corruption in a Typical Racist Right Wing Hate-Filled American Slum City Ruined by Rampant Capitalism and Suppressing Minorities."

After he had gotten the reporter off the phone, Nobile shook his head as he turned to Remo.

"It's getting too close," he said. "We've got to find this nut-case before he blows everything. I need a couple more weeks, without trouble, and I'll have every goddam big Mafia fish in the country in here."

"And when that's all done, what'll you do?" Remo asked.

Rocco Nobile shrugged.

"You know your life's not worth a can of warm beer," Remo said.

"I know," Nobile said. He rubbed his hand through his thick bushy hair. "Oh, I know. They're going to give me a new identity and send me somewhere else, but that's bullshit. Some clown with a hard-on for the government and a peek at the files is going to make himself rich by handing me up. I give myself three months. At least, it's three months I won't have to dye my hair or wear pinky rings or pin-stripe suits." He paused and thought. "Maybe less than three months."

"Then why do you do it?" Remo asked.

"Wouldn't you?"

"I don't know. Maybe. Maybe not. But if I did it, I'd do it for me, not for the government."

"That's the difference between us," Nobile said. He turned around and looked out the window at the tired dull streets of Bay City. He turned down the roar of the rock station which always filled the office. "I guess you could call it a generation gap. But I grew up believing America was worth a life. Even my own."

Remo sat up in his chair. He recognized that. He thought back to Conrad MacCleary, a one-handed man who had brought him into the secret organization CURE. When he lay dying and asked Remo to kill him, he had said the same thing: "America is worth a life."

"I know somebody who said that once," Remo said.

"Federal man?" Nobile asked.

Remo nodded.

"We were taught it," Nobile said. "Can you tell me your friend's name?"

"No. Hell, why not? Conrad MacCleary."

"MacCleary? That one-armed drunken whoremonger?" The words were hard but the face of Rocco Nobile was soft, exuding good memories as he thought back over his life.

Remo nodded.

"Conn and I went through O.S.S. training together." Nobile chuckled. "We both learned that line from one of our meanest, tight-assed bastard instructors that ever lived. We used to make fun of him. Then one day he vanished."

"What happened to him?" Remo asked casually.

"We lost track of him," Nobile said. "And it was World War II, and we had other things to think about. Then I found myself in Germany, doing spy work, and I was captured. They had me in the cellar of an old castle and they were going to kill me. Suddenly, this guy comes into the cellar and orders everybody out. It was my old instructor. What it was was that he'd become a spy behind German lines. He was supposed to be a high-ranking Nazi. Well, he got me out of there. He killed six people on the way. And when he put me on a plane to get me out of Germany, I asked him, 'Aren't you coming?' He said no. He had more work to do. And that was the last I saw of him. That was his line.

'America is worth a life.' Old Graham-Cracker Smith. Dry as dust but a helluva man."

"What was his name?" Remo asked.

"Smith. Harold W. Smith."

"What happened to him?"

"Don't know. He switched to the CIA when it was first set up. He was one of those gray people that you don't notice much but you always get the feeling that he's running things while somebody else takes the credit. Then he just kind of vanished and I heard he had put in his papers. He's probably dead now. Or maybe farming rocks some place up in New Hampshire. Bravest man I ever met."

He looked out the window over his city, musing about old times, then he looked back at Remo, almost in surprise, as if noticing him for the first time.

"What were we talking about? Oh, yeah, MacCleary. He still alive?"

"No," Remo said.

"What happened to him?"

"They sent me to kill him," Remo said.

"Did you?"

"No. I couldn't do it."

"Neither could I. But Harold Smith could've. That was the difference between us. I guess that was the bravery he had that I didn't."

"Sounds like a good man," Remo said. "Someday I'd like to meet him."

When there was no story in the *Post* the next day, Sam Gregory slammed the paper to the floor of his motel room.

"That's it," he snarled.

"What's it?" asked Al Baker nervously. Mark Tolan was at the window, pointing his trigger finger at passing cars. He smiled only when a pedestrian came into range. He practiced seeing how many shots he could squeeze off mentally before the body crumpled and hit the sidewalk. The Lizzard sat at the dressing table, looking at his face for pimples. In front of him was a tumbler filled with Vodka.

"We're going to have to make a different hit," said Gregory. "Something the papers can't ignore."

"It passeth understanding," said Lizzard. "Do we do this thing because 'tis right or because we look for plaudits from the world? That thing is noblest done that is done with no one there to cheer."

"Dammit, I don't want cheers. I want press coverage," Gregory said. "I want the word to go out…we're taking on the Mafia."

"When do we get paid?" asked Baker. "I don't have two cents."

"Nor do I and empty pockets impel a man to dangerous acts," said Lizzard.

"Today," Gregory said in disgust. "I've got money for you all."

"Keep your money," said Tolan from the window.

"Not so fast," said Baker. "It's about time we got paid."

"Truly spoken," said Lizzard. "Truly spoken."

"What do we do next?" Tolan asked.

Gregory looked at the tall husky man. "We're going to hit the Bay City Improvement Association. Rocco Nobile's own club."

"When?"

"Tonight. When those crooked cops drop off their gambling protection money. The press can't ignore that."

"Good," said Tolan. "I'm tired of marking time like this." Yeah, he thought, looking out the window. Life was important and money was important but death was more important, especially when it was the death of bad people. And if there weren't any bad people, yeah, well, then he'd settle for any people. Yeah.

"Marking time?" said Baker. "You shot five people yesterday. Three of them kids."

"Just a warm-up," Tolan said. "Don't you know we're warring on the evil-doers, no matter what disguises they may wear?" He turned toward Baker's eyes. "Bang, bang," he said softly.

"Stop that, will you, looney?" Baker said. "Sam, make him stop doing that."

"Don't call me Sam. I'm The Eraser. You're The Baker. He's The Lizzard."

"And I'm The Exterminator," Tolan said. "Bang, bang." He moved his index finger to point at Lizzard's left temple. "Bang, bang." He pointed his finger at Gregory's forehead. "Bang, bang."

"A looney," said Baker. "A freaking refugee from the rubber room."

"Stop the bickering," Gregory said. "I've got to draw a plan of attack for tonight." He reached for a large yellow pad. From a dresser drawer, he took a box of yellow wooden pencils.

CHAPTER TWELVE

DENISE LOOKED UP FROM the receptionist's desk as Remo came through the door from the mayor's office.

"Lunch?" she said.

He shook his head.

"Dinner? Breakfast in bed?"

"Sorry," Remo said. "Work."

"For that, I need you?"

"An assignment from the Mayor," Remo said.

Denise sat up straighter in her chair.

"He said for you to get as much help as you need. Then get the addresses of all the apartment buildings in town and the phone numbers of the superintendents. Start calling them. Tell them you're from the mayor's office or you're calling for the county nuthouse or whatever you want to tell them. But find out if they've rented an apartment recently to a tall man — way over six feet tall — wearing woman's clothes."

She looked up, nodding her understanding. "The TV who delivered that envelope?"

"You got it," Remo said. "Now this is important. If you find the address, you call me. I'm at the motel over in Jersey City."

"Better than that. When I get it, I'll deliver the address to you."

"I've got a roommate," Remo said.

"Awwww."

"But he goes to bed early," Remo said.

"Ooooh."

"But he's a light sleeper."

"Awwww."

"But I can always rent another room for our conference," Remo said.

"Stop it," she giggled. "You're making me crazy. I'll deliver that address. If I have to visit every apartment in Bay City myself."

Remo touched her on the shoulder. He felt her tingle. "Thanks. It's important."

Her smile almost warmed his back as he left her office. Inside, Rocco Nobile was hanging up the telephone. He shook his head at Remo.

"You can control the news but you can't control the rumors."

"What was that?" Remo asked.

"One of my contacts in California. He'd heard that we were having some trouble."

"What'd you tell him?"

"Just a fire. The usual thing in an old city."

"He buy it?"

"I think so, but we've got to get that lunatic Eraser off the streets."

That afternoon, Remo rented another motel room next to his own and that night, when Rocco Nobile was finished at the office, Remo drove his limousine to the Bay City Arms penthouse apartment. In case anyone was watching, they went into the lobby and entered the elevator. But they stopped at the second floor and walked down a back stairway to the basement, and out a back door where they got into Remo's car.

After Remo had Nobile safe in his motel room, he went to his own room where Chiun was sitting on the floor, waiting. In front of him was the box of ping pong balls.

"Not again, Chiun."

"Again and again until you move correctly. Small errors left unchecked grow into large errors and large errors are what fatalities are made of. And if you are killed, what will people think of me? Hah, there is Chiun who trained someone so badly that he was killed. I do not deserve that, Remo."

"Gee, Chiun, I'm really sorry for your troubles."

"Thank you. Just do not add to them. You have moved badly lately, and we will correct it now."

Chiun was up and put the box of balls on the table alongside him. Remo took his stance ten feet away. Chiun threw. The ball started out far to the right, then hooked sharply just before it reached the wall and swerved back toward Remo's head. Remo put his hand up, edge first, caught the ball and slashed down through it with a hacking motion. The ball split neatly down the center and both halves slammed against the wall with two sharp cracking sounds.

"Good?" said Remo.

"Better," said Chiun. "Again."

He tossed another ball at Remo, this time with an easy deceptive underhand motion. The ball started out low, traveling no more than eight inches above the carpeted floor.

Remo watched the ball, waiting, but it did not rise and he glanced at Chiun with a look of superiority on his face. He looked back down just as the ball swooped and caught Remo under the chin. It fell softly to the rug. Remo rubbed his chin, which smarted from the pain. He bent over, picked up the ball and angrily slammed it with his hand. The ball split. Its two halves slammed against the plywood wall, where their ragged-cut edges bit and stuck.

"Very good," Chiun said. "Get angry at the ball. But not at yourself who is the fool who allowed yourself to be hit."

Two rooms away, the rapping of the ping pong balls against the wall was not lost on Mark Tolan.

"That's it," he said. He pulled a T-shirt over his heavily muscled torso.

"Where are you going?" Sam Gregory asked.

"I'm going over to stick those ping pong paddles up some asses," Tolan said as he walked toward the door. "I already warned them about that racket."

"We've got work to do," Gregory said. "We're going out soon to hit that headquarters."

"I'll be back. Don't start the war without me," Tolan said. As he walked through the door, he thought, Yeah, start the war without me and you've got nobody to fight it. Nobody except a drunk and a fake and a millionaire chart-maker. But when you need the purity of killing, you need Mark Tolan. Yeah.

He pounded on Remo's door with his heavy fist.

"Open up this goddam door."

"It's open," a soft voice replied. Tolan pushed the door open. Inside, he saw a small Oriental man, holding a ping pong ball. The man was wearing a dark green kimono. He was smiling.

"Yes?" the Oriental said.

"Where is he?" Tolan demanded.

"Who?" asked Chiun.

"This wiseass I told to stop playing or else I'd give him his."

Remo stepped forward from the end of the room. "You mean me, ugly?" he said.

Tolan looked around the room. He saw no weapons. And this white guy was skinny. Tolan had him by forty pounds.

"You playing ping pong again?"

"Yeah. You want lessons?"

"No, I come to give you a lesson. I thought I told you to knock it off."

"That was yesterday," Remo said. "This is today."

"Yeah?"

Remo looked at Chiun who shrugged, shaking his head, unable to understand the western mind which did not want people to practice their balance using ping pong balls. If they did not want that, why did westerners bother to invent ping pong balls, Chiun wondered.

"Yeah, sweetheart," Remo said. "Yesterday was yesterday and today is today."

"I told you to stop. I meant for good," Tolan said.

"We'll keep it in mind," Remo said. "Now go away. You're annoying me."

"Yeah?"

"You're really good at dialogue," Remo said.

"Yeah? Well, you're pretty good at lipping off. You want to step outside?"

"Why? Is it nicer out there than in here?"

"More room to mop you up in," Tolan said.

"That's good," said Remo. "I'd give you about a sixty-seven on that one."

"You coming outside or do I mop you up in here?"

Remo thought about Rocco Nobile in the next room. If he heard any noise outside, he might be inclined to look out and someone might just notice him. Remo chose not to go outside.

"You'd better do it here," Remo said. "The afternoon air might chill my ping pong muscles."

Tolan growled and charged into the room. He felt something hook his ankles. He looked back as he was falling. It was the Oriental's foot. The old man had tripped him up. He looked at the Oriental. The old man still had the same simpering smile on his face.

Before he had a chance to reach out and grab that little yellow face in his hands and crush it like an egg, he felt himself being lifted up by the seat of his pants. The skinny white guy had him and was swinging him back and forth. Then he let him go and Tolan swung out through the open door onto the sidewalk in front of the motel room. He felt the skin scraping off his hands and knees as he slid. He heard the door slam behind him.

He rolled over and looked up at the door. The door opened again and a ping pong ball came out and landed in front of Mark Tolan's nose.

He heard the white man's voice. "Come back after you have a chance to practice."

He heard the door lock.

When he stood up and dusted himself off, he again heard the infernal tapping of the ping pong balls off the wall. He started for the door again, but stopped when Sam Gregory came out of his room two doors away. Behind him was Al Baker, looking around carefully before stepping outside. The Lizzard, dressed again in woman's clothes, stood lingering in the doorway.

"Come on," Gregory said. "We've got to leave."

Yeah, it would be fun beating up on the guy, Tolan thought. Taking a ping pong paddle and shoving the handle down the skinny guy's throat. But that wasn't nearly as much fun as spraying the Bay City

Improvement Association with bullets. The skinny white dude would have to wait. Tolan followed Gregory to the car.

Gregory drove.

"Where we going?" Tolan asked.

"To our safe apartment," Gregory said. "We'll time our move from there."

"You got my guns?" Tolan asked.

"The Lizzard has them in his pocketbook," Gregory said.

"Hey, faggot," Tolan called into the backseat. "Don't go getting them smeared with lipstick."

The last ping pong ball had been smashed when there was another knock on Remo's door ninety minutes later, Remo thought it might be the hard-faced guy coming back. He hoped it was. His muscles ached to hit something more substantial than a ping pong ball.

It was Denise. She held a paper in her hands and she smiled when she saw Remo.

She handed it forward.

"Here it is. Three-sixty-four Barrack Street. A big transvestite rented it two days ago."

Remo took the paper and hugged her.

"Oooooh," she said.

"Come on, Chiun, let's go," Remo said. He thought of Rocco Nobile next door. Maybe he should be in at the finish too.

"You going somewhere?" Denise asked. Disappointment crinkled the corners of her eyes.

"Have to now," Remo said. "But there's plenty of time for us."

He got her into her car and then roused Rocco Nobile who was napping, and together with Chiun they drove back into Bay City, toward Barrack Street, toward the Bay City Improvement Association, toward their long-awaited meeting with The Eraser.

CHAPTER THIRTEEN

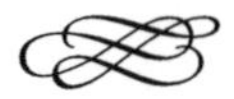

Sam Gregory had titled this one the "Bay City Blast." And he told them, "When we're done here and we've wiped out these Mafia goons, we're going to go across the country. We'll be the stuff legends are made of: Minneapolis Massacre. Birmingham Bloodbath. Tucson Terror. Salinas Slaughter."

"Hey, those are good," said The Baker. "You shoulda been a writer."

"Well, perhaps one day when we're done and we've destroyed the insidious hold of the mob upon our nation," Gregory said.

"Cut the bullshit," Tolan said. "When do we kill somebody?"

As Gregory began to outline his plans, The Lizzard went to his suitcase of clothing. From it he brought out a nun's habit, and after carefully applying makeup that made him look pale and drawn, he began to put it on.

"How do I look?" he asked, spinning around.

"Like a six-and-a-half-foot faggot," said Tolan.

"You look just fine," The Baker said.

"Don't you ever wear man's disguises?" Tolan asked. "Whoever heard of a nun as big as a basketball player?"

"Part of my genius, sir," said The Lizzard. "By the time I walk into that place, I will be so shrunken over that if anyone ever asks, they will remember only a little old nun. The operative word there is 'little.' Such is my genius that I will be absolutely tiny in their memories. Miniscule. Minute."

Gregory looked out the window of the apartment at the Bay City Improvement Association. Its store windows were brightly illuminating the sidewalk in the nighttime darkness.

He told Lizzard, "Now you go over there on some kind of pretext. Tell them anything. Tell them you want to volunteer to help clean up the honky tonks on Barrack Street. But stay there. And when the crooked cops arrive with their gambling money, you come out and give us a sign."

"How do you know they're going to be there tonight?" Baker asked Gregory.

"You told me," Gregory said. "You said this was the night the payoffs were made. Don't you remember?"

"Oh, yeah," said Baker, who had made up the payoff schedule. "This is the squaring away night of the week. That's how the Mafia gambling empire always works. You want me to tell you about it?"

"Later," said Gregory.

"Never," said Tolan.

"All right," Gregory said. "And we'll be watching from up here. When you give us the sign, we'll be over."

After the gaunt man had left the dingy apartment, Tolan said, "I don't trust that faggot."

"You shouldn't call him that, Exterminator," said Gregory. "He's an actor. Dressing up is one of the tools of his trade."

"He likes it too much for it to be just a job," Tolan said. His hands itched to be on a gun, to have people's foreheads down his line of sight, to squeeze and watch them explode away in little fuzzy red chunks. Yeah. He was The Exterminator. Yeah. Legend? Who cared? This beat frying eggs in the diner, that was all he knew.

The three men stood watching from the window as The Lizzard came out of the alley between the tenement buildings, looked around and, when he saw the street was clear, walked across the street to the Improvement Association offices.

"Stoop, you jerk," said Baker. The Lizzard was walking straight up, all six-feet-five of him. Baker wanted to yell out the window at him. That was what he wanted. But more than that, he wanted to be away from here. He had counted on Gregory being good for a big stake so he could go somewhere and try to gamble up some real money. But

Gregory was a little tighter with his money than he had expected. Baker had already forgotten Hawaii and Las Vegas and he had settled down to trying to get to Atlantic City to make his big score. But now, flanked by a madman with a mission on one side and a homicidal maniac on the other, all Al Baker wanted was to get away. With his life.

Just before he reached the far curb, The Lizzard hunched over and then walked slowly to the door of the clubhouse.

Tolan hooted. "Now instead of looking like a six-and-a-half-foot nun," he said, "he looks like a six-and-a-half-foot nun who's all bent over. Where'd you get him?"

"He's doing just fine," Gregory said. His eyes were not on The Lizzard at all. They were on headlines he saw in his mind, huge headlines in huge unnamed papers:

The Eraser Rubs Out the Mob
Bay City Blast
Kokomo Kill
Westport Wipeout
Nuns of Navarone

He thought a moment and scratched that last one. That was somebody else's title. If he ever found a mob-infested American city named Navarone, he would save it till last, until he thought of a good title. The Eraser striking fear into the hearts of the mob.

Inside the headquarters, two secretaries whose salaries were paid personally by Rocco Nobile were compiling a survey of the income and the health needs of the city's residents so Nobile could try to set up a health clinic for preventative medicine. The only other person in the place was Louie, the almost-janitor.

Louie was a borderline moron and had lived largely on handouts and make-work jobs that people gave him. People never expected him to succeed, but Louie knew how to push a broom and he liked the feeling of working and supporting himself, so he made up in energy and dedication what he lacked in technique and quick-wittedness.

As the big nun came through the door, Louie glanced at his watch and realized it was seven o'clock and the bulldog edition of the *Daily News* would be on the stands.

"Hello, Sister lady," he said as he brushed past her to go get a paper. It was the only newspaper Louie read and actually he didn't read all that much of it, just one tiny number on one corner of one page. It was the total mutual handle from a New York racetrack and the last three digits constituted the winning number in the illegal numbers game. Louie played every day.

The two secretaries stood up when they saw the nun, but there was something odd about her and they exchanged glances with each other.

"Oooooh, hello, my dears," The Lizzard said in a high-pitched squeak. "Aren't you both lovely?"

"Thank you, Sister," said the brunette. "Can we help you?"

"It was just the opposite, heh, heh, just the opposite. I was hoping I could help you. You see, I'm at St. Joseph's and we wondered if, perhaps, there was some work we could do to help you in the vital task of rebuilding the city."

"Why don't you sit down, Sister?" the brunette said. She nodded to the blonde secretary that she would handle this. "It's a little late for you to be out, isn't it, Sister?"

"Actually, I received a dispensation from Father Cochran to be out alone on this terrible street."

"Father Cochran? I'm afraid I don't know him. And just where is St. Joseph's?"

Trapped, The Lizzard thought. He improvised. "It's a new church, dear. We're just starting it. But, actually, I didn't come here to talk about myself. Rather, we would like to help in any small way we can."

The brunette secretary didn't know what to make of it. She reached into her desk for an application form. "You wouldn't mind filling this out, would you?"

"Of course not. The longer the better. Nobody here but you two lovelies?"

Louie came back into the Association office on a dead whoop, shouting and pointing at the paper. "I hit! I hit! I had 456 and I hit it in the box! Twenty-five dollars! I hit! I hit!"

"All right, Louie," said the brunette.

The Lizzard stood up quickly. He had heard all he needed to. This man was in here with the numbers play. And besides, it was time for a drink.

"I'll just take this application with me," he said as he snatched the paper from the desk. "And I'll be back tomorrow night."

Without waiting for a reply, he walked out the front door. Behind him, the two girls looked at each other and suppressed laughter. Louie was drawing his finger across the winning number again to make sure that he had won.

Outside on the street. The Lizzard rubbed his forehead three times in the pre-arranged signal.

"That's it," Tolan said joyously. "Let's go kill somebody."

He had a gun in each hand as he walked to the door. Gregory followed him, carrying a Gregory Sur-Shot.

The Baker lingered behind.

"Come on," Gregory said. "Timing is everything."

"Do I have to go?"

"Yes." Gregory looked at the sad expression on Baker's face. "A good job tonight and tomorrow is bonus day for everybody."

Baker brightened appreciably. "Okay, Let's do it."

"Take a gun," Gregory said, pointing toward a small arsenal of weapons on the dresser.

Baker sighed and took the smallest one he could find and stuck it into his jacket pocket. No way he was going to fire it. No way.

They had to run to catch up with Mark Tolan who was marching at doubletime across the street. The plan had been for all of them to talk to The Lizzard and get the lay of the land, but Tolan had had enough of talking. While Gregory and Baker walked toward Lizzard, Tolan marched toward the front door of the Bay City Improvement Association.

"You know where Barrack Street is?" Nobile asked Remo.

"Yeah," said Remo. He spun the car around the corner, making a right-hand turn toward Bay City. The car strained upward on its two inside wheels. Just as it reached the point where it was sure to tip, Remo tromped on the gas pedal, and the sudden forward surge overcame the centrifugal force and brought all four wheels back to the pavement.

"You always drive like this?" Nobile said.

"Yes," said Chiun. "With callous disregard for the lives of people who are worth something, namely me."

"You ain't seen nothing yet," Remo said.

Mark Tolan knew the face of evil when he saw it, no matter how it was painted or disguised. His had looked into evil before, and it could not hide itself from him or from his judgment. The little brunette looked up when he came through the door. She smiled, the same kind of smile she smiled every Sunday at 11 A.M. when she sang in the choir of St. Stephen's Episcopal Church where she was the second alto and was hoping that she would be the first alto next year. She was still smiling when the first Gregory Sur-Shot string of fragmentation slugs ripped into her head.

The blonde secretary was not a choir singer. She was nineteen years old and by the brunette's standards already a fallen woman because she had once let her fiancé touch her *there* and they weren't planning to be married until next year, when he got out of college where he was studying archaeology. She went next, a string of slugs almost severing her neck. She fell onto the table gushing red. Tolan thought, yeah, my favorite color, blondes wearing red.

Louie was sitting at a table in the back of the room and he looked up slowly when he heard the shots and saw the two girls hit and the big goon standing in the doorway. He was enraged because the two girls had been nicer to him than anyone else had ever been and he jumped to his feet and raced at Tolan.

"Bad man, I'm gonna get you," he cried out.

Tolan let him get close, fifteen feet, ten feet. Louie was waving his fists over his head, his puffy face distorted with rage and anger. At eight feet, Tolan squeezed the trigger.

The gun jammed. He squeezed again. It did not fire. Then Louie was on him, his hard little fists flailing at Tolan's face and Tolan didn't like it. For a moment, he thought of running way but then he remembered the other gun in his left hand, the .357 Magnum, and he put it to Louie's right temple and squeezed the trigger. This one fired and Louie dropped to the freshly linoleumed floor.

Tolan ran to the back of the office hoping there were more people there. But there weren't. He turned and ran back toward the street. He grabbed a handful of pencils from his pocket, and with one wrench broke off their eraser ends and dropped them onto the floor. On the street, he met The Eraser, The Baker and the Lizzard.

"All done," said Tolan. "Let's go."

The four men ran back up the steps of the tenement building where they kept an apartment, just as Remo's car turned the corner. He pulled up in front of the Bay City Improvement Association, as Gregory and his three accomplices began to look out the window. Remo was scanning the windows on the other side of the street.

"Hey, I know him," Tolan said. "That's the dip with the ping pong balls."

Remo looked up at their apartment and for one chill moment, it seemed to Gregory that his eyes had locked with those of the hard-faced man in the street.

Behind Remo, Chiun and Nobile had gone to the Association offices.

"Oh, my God," Remo heard Nobile say.

He turned to see the mayor bent over the body of Louie near the doorway. Chiun was gesturing to Remo to go after the shooters.

"Nobile," Tolan said upstairs. "I can get him from here."

"No. We want him to sweat a little," Gregory said. "First his drug trade, then his numbers business. Next is him, but let him wait."

Baker saw Remo look in the Association headquarters. He saw the thin man's fist clench. Remo turned and ran across the street toward them. His face was twisted with anger.

"We better get out of here," Baker said.

"I think you're right," Gregory said.

"Let's shoot it out with him," Tolan said.

"Later," said Gregory. "We'll get him on our terms."

The four men went through a back window and down the fire escape. Their rented car had been parked in a vacant lot behind the old tenement building.

When Remo kicked in the apartment door, they were gone. He

looked out the back window and saw only the taillights of the car pulling around a building and into the street.

"Damn," he said. "Damn."

Back at the Association headquarters, Chiun handed Remo three broken pencils.

"I thought you would want these," he said.

CHAPTER FOURTEEN

IT WAS ONE THE TV ELEVEN O'CLOCK NEWS.

The three major New York channels carried brief pieces on the killings. They described how Mayor Rocco Nobile, making his usual nightly visit to the club, had come on the scene only seconds after the shootings.

"It was two young juveniles," the stations quoted Nobile as saying, "I ran after them, but they were too fast for me and they got away." He described them as Hispanic youths, perhaps five-foot-six or -seven, wearing yellow nylon windbreakers. He pledged an all-out police effort to apprehend the perpetrators.

There was no mention of the erasers dropped at the scene and nothing to tie in the shootings with the fire near the waterfront the day before.

Sam Gregory and his three cohorts watched the news together. Gregory reacted in cold fury.

"What do you have to do to get on the TV news?" he wondered aloud.

"Kill the mayor," said Tolan. But his mind wasn't on killing the mayor. It was on the nutcase with the ping pong balls. His hands still hurt where he had hit the sidewalk in front of the nutcase's room, and Tolan owed him one. If the man was associated with Mayor Nobile, so much the better. Maybe he was a Mafia bodyguard. He had dark hair and eyes. He might be Italian. Yeah, Mafia. He was sure of it. Yeah.

Tolan looked around the room at Baker, still sweating and nervous. At Lizzard, who had changed out of his nun's habit. At Gregory, who kept drumming his fingers on the table top.

"Maybe I should call the TV channels," Gregory said.

"Naah. They won't believe you anyway," said Baker.

"And besides, they might trace the call and find us," Lizzard said.

"Let them," Tolan said. "Nothing nicer than shooting a left-wing pinko newspaper reporter."

They sat in the room and watched reruns of "The Honeymooners," "The Odd Couple" and "Twilight Zone." Lizzard drank vodka. Gregory finally fell asleep and Tolan grabbed the other two and motioned for them to follow him into the bathroom.

"Here's our chance to do something for The Eraser," Tolan said.

"Yeah?" asked Baker suspiciously. He did not like being in the bathroom with The Exterminator.

"If we do it, can we get another bottle of Vodka from room service?" asked The Lizzard.

"Sure," said Tolan with a big fake smile. "And you'll get paid an extra bonus tomorrow, Baker."

"What is it?" Baker asked.

"Those two guys we saw tonight at the club. The skinny one and the old Chink. They're next door."

"Next door, here?" Baker asked. Already, he didn't like it.

"Right," Tolan said. "And if we get them, then Rocco Nobile will be a piece of cake."

"Good. You go get 'em," Baker said.

"I need your help," said Tolan.

"Two of them, we ought to get two bottles of vodka from room service," said The Lizzard.

"I'll get you three," said Tolan. "I'll go get them myself so you don't have to wait for no waiter."

The Lizzard had no problem with that. And when Baker was told by Tolan that he'd get Gregory not only to double but triple Baker's pay and then it was off to Las Vegas for a life of baccarat and broads, Baker agreed. Particularly, since it was so simple and safe.

The door to the skinny guy's room was probably unlocked. All they had to do was to sneak into the other room after the men were asleep.

Flick on the light switch inside the door and flee. The two men, the skinny one and the old Chink, would come rushing after them. And Mark Tolan would be in the parking lot, waiting. He would level them both. That would get rid of Rocco Nobile's bodyguards and also make sure that the work of The Eraser and the Rubout Squad made the newspapers.

"That's all we got to do?" asked Baker. "Open the door, reach in and turn on the light and then run like hell?"

"Right," said Tolan. "I'll handle the rest."

"Triple pay?" asked Baker.

"I guarantee it. If Gregory won't give it to you, you can have mine."

Baker rubbed his hands. "Let's go," he said.

"Could we get one bottle of vodka first?" asked Lizzard.

"No," said Tolan.

The Exterminator was in position. He was crouched between two cars, directly opposite from Remo and Chiun's room. His Gregory Sur-Shot was in his hand. Baker and Lizzard waited outside the window, making sure no one was awake inside the room.

Yeah, it would be easy, Tolan thought. Lights on, they run and he nails the two frigging ping pong players as they came out. Ping pong players deserved to die, yeah, almost as much as Mafia thugs and evil-doers. All he had to do was make sure that The Lizzard and The Baker got out of the way first, and he wasn't all too worried about that. After all, accidents happened. They had signed on for, yeah, a dirty dangerous business when they signed on to go to war against the Mafia.

He watched as the two men skulked along the concrete strip of sidewalk outside the door of the ping pong players' room. Tolan wondered who they were. They were driving Rocco Nobile around so they weren't just ping pong players. But ping pong was big in China and China was starting to deal with the United States and the old guy was a Chink so that was it, yeah, they were Mafia businessmen putting together a big new drug deal with China and, yeah, he would be the guy to kill them before the deal could get off the ground. The thought of doing a public service made Tolan smile a little, the way he used to smile in Nam when he was doing another public service by shooting anything that was yellow and moved.

Baker and Lizzard were outside the door now. It took the two of them to have the courage of one man, Tolan knew. He saw Baker reach for the doorknob. He saw the door open slightly. He saw Lizzard's long skinny arm snake through the crack and reach inside for the light switch.

Then he saw Lizzard catapult into the room, banging the door wide open with his body as he went. Baker dropped the doorknob as if it were hot. He tried to turn, to run, to flee but suddenly he was yanked into the room also, as if he had been a paper clip on the end of a rubber band, stretched tight, then suddenly released.

The door slammed closed.

And The Exterminator knew something was wrong. Yeah. He ran back to his room and shook Sam Gregory awake.

"What is it?" Gregory said.

"They got them. The Lizzard and Baker. We've got to get out of here."

"Who? What?"

"I'll tell you about it when we drive," said Tolan. "Let's go."

"Dammit, Chiun, did you have to do that?" Remo pointed at the two bodies in the corner.

"No, I did not have to do that. I am sure that they were just sneaking into our room in the middle of the night to ask us to donate to the Blue Cross."

"Red Cross," Remo said.

"So I did not have to do that. I could have waited for several hours until the brass band arrived and you finally woke up to do something about these two."

"I was awake," Remo said. "I heard them. I was going to let them get in so we could find out who they were."

"Who they were is very simple. The big thing with no meat on his bones was the thing who dressed up as a woman."

"And the other one?"

"I have no knowledge of that one," Chiun said.

"Did they have weapons?"

"No."

"I wonder how they found us," Remo said. He remembered something. "The Mayor," he said and ran to the door connecting their room with the mayor's. Rocco Nobile was sound asleep, unharmed.

Remo went back into his own room.

"Maybe they were registered in the motel," he said.

"You will not find out by suggesting it to me," Chiun said. "I am not a room clerk."

Remo went to the door to check at the front desk. He looked over his shoulder at Chiun who was back on his sleeping mat at the end of the room.

"Remember, you clean these up yourself," Remo said.

"One each," Chiun said.

"You do them both," Remo said.

"We will discuss it in the morning when I wake up. If ever I am allowed to sleep."

The desk clerk remembered them. There were four men in the room, only two doors from Remo's. No, he didn't really know what they looked like. They kind of kept to themselves.

When Remo got back, the room was empty. He went through it quickly, but except for a pocketbook containing women's makeup, there was nothing.

When he returned to his own room, he heard voices inside the room of Rocco Nobile. He moved quickly inside and saw the mayor talking to a large uniformed police captain. The conversation was finished and the captain was leaving.

Nobile waited until he had gone before turning to Remo and swearing softly.

"What's wrong?" Remo asked.

"Those dumb bastards. They traced the pencils and they didn't bother to tell me about it till now."

"So what'd they find out?"

"The pencils were bought at the Cole Stationery Supplies, except they weren't really bought. A big guy came in and took the box and refused to pay for them. He was so big and nasty-looking that the owner just let it happen. He was afraid to call the cops."

"Big and nasty-looking? Anything else?" Remo asked.

"They described him as a big guy. Dark hair and muscular. Always scowling. Had glinty eyes and looked like a psycho."

Remo nodded. He knew the man. It was the pest who had come to their door to stop the ping pong practice. And Remo had just let him get away.

CHAPTER FIFTEEN

THE TRACTOR TRAILER WAS PARKED around the corner from City Hall. It took up parking spots at three meters and when the policeman on the beat first saw it at 10:20 A.M., he realized he had a problem.

Since the red flags were up on three meters, did he give it three parking tickets or one parking ticket? A difficult question but, under its last mayor, the Bay City police department had made it a point to send all their patrolmen to leadership training classes, and since he had graduated third in the class, the policeman did not hesitate more than a few seconds. He wrote two parking tickets, neatly halving the difference between regulations and compassion which was one of the things they learned in leadership class.

He also looked for the driver in the two luncheonettes on the block but did not find him. He therefore made another leadership decision. If he came back at 11 A.M. and the truck was still parked there, he would write one more additional ticket. That would total three tickets for three parking spaces. He regarded this as a neat solution to a complicated problem and told himself that neither the chief nor the president of the Patrolmen's Benevolent Association would have been able to figure it out, because they were not part of the new breed of cops.

At ten to eleven, Sam Gregory, who had been leaning on a light pole across the street from City Hall, reading a newspaper, saw the mayor's car go into the City Hall parking lot. He started to walk back to the truck.

At two minutes to eleven, the patrolman again turned the corner at the end of the street. He saw the truck still parked there. He had his ticket pad open as he walked down the block toward it.

As he drew near the truck, the back doors of the vehicle swung open wide. Two heavy metal ramps clanged out of the truck onto the street. The cop stopped. It couldn't be.

He blinked and looked again.

It was.

An Army tank, painted olive drab, chugged down the steel ramps. The ramps buckled under the weight of the tank, but the war machine reached the pavement in one piece. It totaled a Volkswagen in the parking spot behind the truck, then made a U-turn and headed toward City Hall.

The policeman wondered what to do. Leadership training hadn't covered tanks. Maybe he should call headquarters. On the other hand, maybe it was a tank for a parade. But if they were going to have a parade, they should have told him about it. Leadership required that. It wasn't Armed Forces Day. It wasn't even Memorial Day. But who the hell knew? Everybody had parades nowadays. The Germans and the Italians and the Irish and the Puerto Ricans. Who knew? Maybe it was the annual parade of the Palestine Liberation Organization. They might feature tanks. He decided he would not embarrass himself by calling headquarters and appearing dumb. He would wait until he saw what happened. He put his ticket book away and walked slowly after the tank as it lumbered down the middle of the block.

It turned the corner into the street fronting City Hall.

The driver of a white diesel Oldsmobile saw it coming at him and drove up on the curb, smashing into a parking meter to avoid getting hit. When the car's engine died, the driver realized it was the first time in weeks that his ears hadn't hurt from the motor's noise.

The driver shook a fist at the tank. He was about to charge it and scream at the driver when he realized the driver wouldn't or couldn't hear him. He continued shaking his fist. He wondered what else he could do to vent his anger, when he saw the turret of the tank open and a dark-faced man with a swoop of thick black hair over his forehead stick his head out. He was carrying guns in both hands. The Oldsmobile driver decided not to argue with the guns. The eyes of the man in the tank turret were darting little pinpoints, flashing as he looked from side to side.

The policeman who had been trailing the tank reached the corner just as the tank turned in the middle of the street so that it was facing City Hall.

The tank stood still but its motor kept chugging. The Oldsmobile driver realized that the tank idled more quietly than his diesel did.

"Hey," the cop called. "Hey, you in the tank." He had decided that this was no parade, and even if it was, the assembly spot sure wasn't the middle of the street in front of City Hall. The man in the top of the tank turned toward him.

"Hey, you can't park there," the cop yelled at Mark Tolan.

"No?" said Tolan. The cop drew his ticket book from his right hip. Tolan shot him in the left side of the chest.

Inside City Hall, Remo and Chiun were in the mayor's office with Rocco Nobile, who was hanging his jacket on the old-fashioned coat rack in the corner.

They all heard the noise out front and went to the window. As they looked out through the large double panes of glass, they saw the cannon on the front of the tank lift up, until it was pointing at them like a long accusing ringer. On top of the tank, half in half out, Remo recognized the looney who hated ping pong. Behind him, in the street, was a dead policeman. Remo gritted his teeth, then turned to Chiun, but Chiun was not there. As Remo continued turning, he saw Chiun race across the room, dragging Mayor Nobile to the floor.

"Down, Remo," called Chiun and Remo hit the floor just as an artillery shell slammed into the side of the building just below the picture window. Brick and mortar flew into the room, dropping on Remo's body. A foot-wide hole opened in the front of the building. The glass above Remo trembled and cracked, and glass shards fell onto his body.

"To the door," Chiun hissed.

Remo moved toward the big oaken doors. Behind him he could hear the fault sound of another shell before it slammed into the wall of the building with an ear-splitting crash.

He pulled open the door and Chiun dragged Rocco Nobile out of the office. Secretaries were scattering. Remo closed the oaken doors and turned to Chiun.

"Get him out of here, Chiun," said Remo.

"Where are you going?"

"After those nuts," Remo said. "You get to the parking lot and get him out of here."

Chiun nodded. Remo moved out into the marble-floored hallway. Behind him he heard another shell rip the front of the building. It had been years since he had heard tank shells exploding around him.

When he got to the front steps of the building, the tank was still firing away at the mayor's office. Remo saw that the hard-faced man had gone from the tank turret and when he got outside, he saw the man, waving two guns, running down the block on the left side of the building.

That would take him to the parking lot, Remo realized. That could have been the plan all along. To drive the mayor out of his office by tank and then pick him off with a bullet in the parking lot.

Remo followed the man. As he passed under the open windows of the mayor's second floor office, another shell exploded above him and rocks and debris fell down toward his body. He dodged the flying rocks and got to the sidewalk just in time to see the hard-faced Mark Tolan climb the fence into the parking lot.

Remo raced after him.

Chiun led the mayor down the back steps of the city hall building to the parking lot.

Before he stepped outside, he looked carefully both ways. No one was in the lot except the parking attendant with the rum nose and plaid shirt, who was sitting in a city car, reading *Playboy* magazine.

Chiun nodded to Nobile and they walked quickly toward the mayor's car.

Just as Chiun opened the door, he heard a voice behind them.

"Hey, Chinkie, that's as far as you go."

He turned to see the brooding dark-haired man staring at them. He had a pistol in each hand. Chiun moved in front of the mayor and hissed to him softly, "Into the car and down."

Nobile moved back from Chiun and into the car, trying to fit himself onto the floor on the passenger's side. His hand reached up to unlock the door, and he pulled the handle so that the door was open, in case he had to roll through it.

"That won't do any good," Mark Tolan said to Chiun. He had a smile on his face, a twisted smile that involved only his mouth. His eyes remained cold. "I'll shoot right through you to get to him."

"Have to shoot through me first," said a voice from behind Tolan.

Tolan wheeled just as Remo lightly vaulted the low cyclone fencing which surrounded the parking lot. He was ten feet from Tolan.

"Yeah," Tolan said. He savored the moment. Three people to kill and more maybe might come. Yeah, it was going to be a good day. A good day for dying.

"Well, well, well," he said. "If it ain't the other ping pong player."

"Are you The Eraser?" Remo asked.

"No. I'm The Exterminator."

"Cute," said Remo. "Any other fancy names?"

"The two guys you killed. That was The Lizzard and The Baker."

"Then who the hell's The Eraser?" Remo demanded.

"In the tank," Tolan said. "What's your name? Ping Pong?"

Remo looked across the ten feet of distance and smiled and his smile was colder and more heartless than Tolan's.

"Me?" Remo intoned the words softly. "I am created Shiva, the Destroyer; death, the shatterer of worlds. You don't know what that means, do you?"

"No," said Tolan.

"It means you're done, axe-face."

They should have been in the parking lot by now, Sam Gregory realized, so he put his tank into "drive" and began to chug forward, around the corner back toward the lot, where he was supposed to pick up The Exterminator. He heard a few cartridges pinging off the heavy armor of the tank and smiled. Almost all done.

Remo moved across the blacktop toward Mark Tolan. Tolan let him come. The closer the target, the bigger the hole. At five feet, he fired with the Gregory Sur-Shot in his right hand.

And missed.

Remo went down below the fragmenting slugs as if he had slipped down an open elevator shaft. Then he was on his feet again and before Tolan could squeeze off another round, he felt the gun slapped from his hand and heard its metallic clink on the pavement.

As Remo raised his hands toward Tolan, the burly man lifted his left hand and fired his .357 Magnum at Remo but even as he pressed the trigger, he knew it would miss, because Remo was no longer in front of him. The bullet fired with a loud crack. Tolan could see instantly crazed glass where the slug splintered its way through the windows of three parked automobiles.

Tolan felt a tap on his shoulder and, as he turned, the Magnum was knocked from his hand. And the crazy ping pong player was behind him and Tolan thought, yeah, well, he's good at dodging bullets but I'm fifty pounds heavier than he is and I'm going to tear his throat out with my hands and, yeah, if I like it, maybe I'll switch to using my hands from now on and he reached up and put his two big ham fists around the thin man's throat.

"Destroyer, huh? Try this destroyer," Tolan said. He began to squeeze with all the power in his bulky muscles. Remo did not stop smiling.

If he hadn't seen it with his own eyes, Sam Gregory would never have believed it.

He stopped the tank in the middle of the street near the parking lot. He saw Tolan inside the lot with his hands around the neck of a thin dark-haired man. It was the man he'd seen the night before at the Bay City Improvement Association.

The thin man slowly raised his hands and pressed his thumbs into Tolan's wrists and Tolan's hands separated and dropped from the man's throat.

The thin man was talking to Tolan but Gregory couldn't hear what he said.

"...You kill those little girls at headquarters last night?" Remo asked.

Tolan did not answer. He was trying desperately to make his hands move but they felt as if they had been dipped into plaster of Paris and left to dry for six days.

"I asked you a question," Remo said. He punched an index finger softly into Tolan's ear lobe.

"Yes, yes," Tolan shrieked. He had never known an ear lobe could hurt like that.

"And that poor Chinese family?"

"Drug dealers," Tolan gasped. "Yes. I did it."

"You're The Exterminator," Remo said. "When I'm done with you, there won't be enough left for roach paste."

Gregory put his eyes closer to the narrow slit through which a tank commander could see the battlefield in front of him. As he watched, he saw the bulky muscular Tolan being lifted in the air, above the head of the thin man. The thin man whirled gently, not with any obvious muscular effort as with a shot putter or discus thrower, but as if he were doing a gentle dance step, and then Tolan was slamming through the air. His body traveled twenty feet and then, like a spear, it went headfirst through the front windshield of the car owned by the city's Deputy Director of Community Improvement.

Tolan hit with a shudder, like a javelin sticking into the ground, and then the lower part of his body buckled and his knees banged down on the hood of the new Mercedes.

Gregory shuddered inside the safe confines of his tank. He hadn't thought making war on the Mafia was going to be easy, but this was ridiculous. It was time to retire to reconsider his situation.

Then he saw something else. There was an old Oriental standing in front of a car on the far side of the parking lot and as the Oriental moved away, behind him Gregory could see Mayor Rocco Nobile crawling out of the car.

He could not pass up the opportunity. Gregory wheeled the tank turret around. Here was his chance. He could put a shell into the Mafia mayor's midsection.

But as he lowered the barrel of the cannon into position, his eyes met those of the Oriental. And while their eyes locked, the ancient yellow man began walking across the parking lot toward the tank and Gregory realized what he was looking at. He was looking into the eyes of death and at that moment, he decided that from here on, it would be live and let live between himself and the Mafia and all these strange people they had working for him.

He put the tank in drive gear again and began rumbling down the street toward the city's piers. Behind him, straggled out, was a crowd of city policemen, ineffectively firing pistol bullets at the huge olive drab machine.

Nobile ran up behind Remo and Chiun.

"Is that The Eraser?" he asked.

"I guess so," Remo said. "I can't keep track of all these ninnies and their names." He turned to Chiun. "We'd better go after him." He nodded to the mayor. "You stay here."

"Not on your life."

"No. On yours. And tell those cops to stop shooting. They're liable to hit something. Like us," Remo said. He and Chiun hurdled the low fence and ran off after the speeding tank.

"Stop that goddamn shooting," Nobile yelled at a police captain.

The captain nodded as if that was the sensible command he had been waiting for since the start of this incident and shouted for his men to holster their guns. The firing stopped and the captain looked back toward Nobile for approval, but the mayor had already darted back into his car, started it up, and was driving down the street after the tank and Remo and Chiun.

He wondered what kind of men they were and where in the government they had come from. What they did, he had never seen done before, and it made him feel a little better to know that they were on his country's side.

Behind him, the police captain was confused. He had not done all that well in leadership class and now he did not know what to do. Should he follow the mayor or wait for further orders? He decided to follow at a safe distance. No one could fault him for that. He hoped.

The tank got to the waterfront before Remo and Chiun did. Sam Gregory stuck his head out of the turret and saw the white man and the Oriental following him. They were only half a block away. Behind them came speeding Rocco Nobile's car.

It was a good thing he had thought of everything, Gregory realized as he clambered up out of the turret, jumped to the ground and ran down the concrete pier.

An eighteen-foot power boat was tied up to one of the large pilings and Gregory untied the line, then dropped down into the boat. The motor started up instantly, as he turned the key and pressed the automatic starter.

He pulled away from the pier twenty feet, then let the motor idle.

Remo and Chiun stood on the edge of the pier, looking down at him. Rocco Nobile's car screeched to a stop, and the mayor ran up between the other two men. All looked out at Sam Gregory.

He shook his fist at them.

"Maybe you win this round," he called. "But I'll be back. I'm coming after you. The Eraser will get you all."

"Oh, no," said Remo. He moved toward the edge of the pier to dive in and swim after the boat, but Chiun restrained him with a hand on his arm.

Gregory saw Remo poised at the edge and threw the boat into high speed and surged away toward the open waters of the Hudson River.

Remo looked at Chiun with surprise. "Why not?" he said. "I don't want to have to deal with him again later."

"Never send a boy to do a boom's job," Chiun said.

He scurried back toward the tank, hopped up on its side and vanished inside. As Remo and Nobile watched, the turret began to swing around. Then the cannon lowered until it was pointing out at the fleeing power boat.

The roar as the cannon exploded crackled in their ears. They looked out into the river and saw the boat of Sam Gregory explode. Wood and metal and body flew high into the air, as the tank shell ripped into it. As they kept watching, the waters slowly subsided into their normal thick stillness. All that was left visible were a few chunks of heavy wood.

Nobile looked at Remo as Chiun returned to their side.

"It looks like The Eraser's been erased," Nobile said.

There was only one thing left to do.

They had done a pretty good job of covering up the earlier incidents but there was no covering this one up, Remo knew. Bay City was zero as far as a safe city was concerned.

While Rocco Nobile began telling the late-arriving policemen what to do, Remo went to a pay telephone on the end of the pier, and dialed Harold W. Smith's number.

When the CURE director came on the telephone, Remo said, "Move now. We blew it."

"What happened?"

"We got The Eraser and that whole gang of clowns. But they had a tank and they bombed City Hall, and I think every goon in this city is probably packing now. If you want to get any of them, you'd better move fast."

"Sounds like your usual neat job," Smith said.

"Smitty, I don't have time for your sarcasm. Are you going to move or not?"

"I already have," Smith said. "A federal task force is already in town, picking up everybody in sight." He paused. "What about Nobile?"

"He's okay, Smitty."

"Did he find out anything about you? About us?"

"No," Remo said.

"Good. Then why don't you just get him out of town safely? He'll know where to hide and what to do."

Remo knew the alternative. If Rocco Nobile had found out about CURE, Remo's assignment would have been quite different. It would have been simply to kill Rocco Nobile, lest he ever say anything about CURE.

"Sounds good to me, Smitty. See ya."

When he hung up and turned around, Rocco Nobile was standing there.

He nodded toward the telephone.

"Checking in?" he asked.

"Yeah. They already started picking up the mobbies in town."

"Good," said Nobile. "I guess it's time for Rocco Nobile to vanish."

"Yeah, it is," Remo said. They walked together toward the mayor's car. Chiun already sat in the back seat, doing his finger tapping exercise for digital dexterity.

At the door of the car, Nobile looked up at the taller Remo.

"I couldn't help but overhear," he said. "Did you say 'Smitty' on the telephone?"

"'Smitty?'" Remo said. "Why would I say 'Smitty?'" He pretended to think for a moment. "Oh, I know what you heard. I said this was a shitty deal. You misheard me."

He looked hard at Rocco Nobile who stared back, and then let his face relax into a smile.

"I guess you're right," he said.

"Good," said Remo. "I'm glad you feel that way."

And he was.

EXCERPT

If you enjoyed *Bay City Blast,* maybe you'll like *Missing Link,* too. It's the thirty-ninth Destroyer novel, now available as an ebook and as a paperback.

Missing Link

HIS NAME WAS REMO and he was going to do something about pollution in America.

He stood on a hill looking down at three tall smokestacks that jutted up into the sky, puffing out wisps of thin white smoke. It was coal smoke, Remo knew, but it had been washed and filtered and processed until it was cleaner than the smoke from oil furnaces. The cleansing process had raised the price of using coal until it was higher than that of using oil bought from the Arabs. But it was all America had — high-priced oil or equally high-priced coal. Nuclear power was dead in the water. A small accident in which not one person was injured — no person had ever been injured in a nuclear accident in America — had been turned into the scare story of the century by the media, and by the time it was over, the drive toward nuclear power was scuttled. Remo thought it was sad that the country that had developed and pioneered nuclear power someday probably would be the only country in the industrial world not to use it. The marchers had won again.

They were the same marchers who had welcomed the Vietcong victory in Vietnam and so weakened America's will that the United States pulled out of the Far East and let it be overrun by the communists. A long night of terror had descended over that part of the world. In Cambodia the illiteracy rate had reached 99 percent because everybody who could read or write had been murdered. It was a country with six doctors for six million people. Somehow, the marchers had nothing to say about that.

Remo had decided a long time before that America had lost more than face when it quit the war in Vietnam. It had lost America; it had lost its spirit. Formosa was given up, Iran was lost. In southern Africa, America had made it clear that the only government it would recognize would be a government made up of Communist terrorists — no matter how the people of that region voted. A college professor whose primary qualification was that she hated America had gone to Russia to receive an award from the Communists and said that all the talk about Soviet persecution of dissidents was a smokescreen to cover up America's persecution of dissidents. And then she had gone back to her publicly paid position on the faculty of a state-supported college.

So much pollution, Remo thought, as he looked down into the small valley at the five thousand people who were camped outside the fences of the small coal-burning electrical generation plant. He turned to the small Oriental next to him and said sadly, "Chiun, it's all over."

"What is?" the Oriental said. He was only five feet tall, almost a foot shorter than Remo. He continued to look down at the crowd, the thin wisps of white beard and hair around his ears puffing occasionally in a stray breeze.

"America," Remo said. "We're done."

"Does this mean we are finally leaving to find work elsewhere?" Chiun asked. He looked toward Remo who was still staring down at the crowd. "I have told you many times there is no shortage of countries that would be glad to have two premier assassins performing for them." Chiun's voice was high-pitched but strong, a voice that seemed too strong to come from a man who appeared to be eighty years old and frail. The old Oriental wore a bright white brocade kimono and despite the summer heat of Pennsylvania, he did not sweat.

"No," Remo said. "It does not mean that we are going to look for work elsewhere. It's just kind of sad that no matter what we do, America is shot."

"I have never understood this," Chiun said. "You act as if America were something special, but it is not special. It is just another country. Think of the grandeur that was Greece, the glory that was Rome, gone in the mists of time. All that is left is men who dance with each other and women who cook spaghetti. Think of the pharaohs and their empires. Think of the blond Macedonian. All gone. Should America be different?"

"Yes," Remo said stubbornly.

"You can explain why?"

"Because this country is free. All those other places you mentioned, there was no freedom. But here people are free. And we're being conquered from inside. We're being torn up by Americans."

"That is the way it is with freedom," Chiun said. "Give people freedom and many of them will use it to fight you."

"So what's the answer?" Remo asked. "Take away freedom?"

The wizened old man looked up at the sky before replying. A lone chicken hawk patrolled the bright white skies. "The House of Sinanju has been in many nations for many centuries," he said.

"I know," said Remo. "Please, no history lectures."

"All I wish to say was that this was the first country I had ever learned of which seemed to be run by caprice and whimsy. It is as if the tiniest minority runs this nation, and it is always that minority which hates the country most."

"I know that," Remo said. "So remove the freedom? That's the answer?"

"No," Chiun said. "Remove the freedom and you will be conquered from outside. Keep the freedom and you will be destroyed from inside."

"So there's no hope," Remo said.

"None at all," Chiun said. "All nations die. The only thing wrong with your nation's death is that it will be inglorious. Better to die before the sword than before the germ." He looked down again at the five thousand people lounging around before the electric company gates, a few of them shouting slogans and singing. "Take heart with one thing, though," he said.

"What's that?" Remo asked.

"Those germs down there. When this country gives way to whatever will follow it, be assured that they will be the first to go."

Remo shook his head. "It all makes you feel hopeless."

"No, no," Chiun said quickly. "We have our art. The fullness of our lives comes from within. It requires nothing else."

"Except targets," Remo said.

"That is true," Chiun said. "I stand corrected. Assassins need targets."

Suddenly Remo was angry and he waved his hand at the marchers milling around below and said, "There should be enough targets there to satisfy anyone."

"I will wait for you here," Chiun said. "Enjoy yourself. But restrain your anger."

"I will," Remo said as he moved quickly down the hill. This was the fifth day the electric plant had been shut down by the pickets who surrounded it. The demonstrators had also made a daily run at the fence surrounding the plant and each day had been held off by the beleaguered town and plant police. But this day was different, Remo had heard. He had gotten word from Upstairs that guns and explosives had been shipped in to the demonstrators.

With the plant closed down, one hundred thousand families had been without electricity for five days. No refrigeration, no electric lights, no television and no radio. Hospitals were using emergency generators to perform major surgery and if any of those generators failed, people would die because there were no more backup systems.

The crowd around the electric plant was like a small declivity in marshland. When the tide came in, it filled, and when the tide went out, it emptied. Except that the television cameras were the water pressure that filled and emptied this pool of people. When the TV cameras were on, they charged the fence and chanted, and when the cameramen had gone, the pickets pulled back away from the fence, leaving behind a landscape littered with broken frisbees, sandwich wrappers, plastic Big Mac containers, the stubs of hand-rolled cigarettes, and the remnants of their signs opposing dirty air and "the polluting coal interests."

This was the low tide time. Remo moved through the large crowd, which hung out in lethargic groups, many of them lying on their backs working on their suntans. Others shared beer. Vendors were selling sunflower seeds. A hundred feet away, a half-dozen uniformed policemen guarded the plant gates, but even they stood relaxed, knowing that the absence of TV camera had lulled everything into a kind of truce.

Remo did not expect to find the person he was looking for. No one looked at him as he walked around through the small clusters of people.

"Hey, man, got a smoke?" somebody asked him.

"No," Remo said.

"Come on, gimme a smoke," the man said. He grabbed Remo's shoulder. Remo turned to look at him. He was a thin man in his mid-forties wearing a powder-blue polyester leisure suit and white patent leather shoes. Remo wondered what he was doing there. Weren't revolutionaries supposed to stop revolting when they got older? They weren't supposed to switch from jeans to leisure suits and keep doing the same old thing in different clothes.

"Aren't you a little old for this?" Remo asked. He disengaged the man's hand from his shoulder. The man felt his hand go numb. But it did not hurt; that would come later.

"Yeah, I suppose so, but what the hell, this is where the chickies are."

Remo shrugged.

"But you need grass to score," the man said. "You really do. Come on. I gotta make some grass."

"I'd like to see you all making grass," Remo said. "From underneath."

"Owwww, my hand hurts. What'd you do to it?"

"Enjoy it," Remo said. "It's organic pain. The real thing."

"You're not funny," the man said. He wore a vasectomy pin in his lapel. "What are you doing here anyway?"

"I'm looking for Janie Baby," Remo said. She was an internationally known folk singer who had made a fortune in America, then moved to London where she unleashed a continuing series of broadsides at racist, imperialist, war-mongering America. She had stayed in London five years, until the British had raised their tax rate into the ninety percent range, whereupon she had moved back to America and married an attorney who had gained notoriety by defending protest leaders in the Sixties. He was called the intellectual force behind the protest movement, which was not all that difficult, considering that most of the protesters regarded logic as a middle-class white American trick to enslave the blacks and the poor.

"She said she's coming back later. She's probably in her room in town," the man said. He tried to rub his hand, but when he touched it, it hurt and he made a grimace of pain.

"Thanks," Remo said. "Watch out for that hand." In her room in town? Remo doubted it. The shutdown of electricity would have shut down the air conditioning in her suite and in the extreme summer heat, she was not going to be in any uncooled room if she didn't have to be.

Remo trotted back up the hill and collected Chiun who seemingly had not moved a muscle since Remo had left. They drove back into the small town of Clairburg and Remo stopped alongside a policeman doing traffic duty.

"Officer," he called.

The policeman flinched as if expected to be attacked. His hand crept toward his holster. Then he saw Remo and relaxed at the sight of an adult.

"Yes," he said.

"With all the power off," Remo said, "where's the nearest motel with air conditioning?"

"Let's see," the cop said. He thought for a moment. Remo could see the man's lips moving. "The nearest one'd be the Makeshift Motel, four miles outside town. On Route 90. Go straight, this turns right into it. You a reporter?"

"No," Remo said.

"Good. I hate reporters."

"Don't weaken and don't falter," Remo said as he drove off.

The Makeshift Motel was only five minutes away, spread out alongside the road like four ranch homes that had decided to go through life together. Remo parked in the oversized lot, and Chiun waited in the car while the younger man went into the office.

There was a blonde young woman in the office, flanked by two plastic ferns. She wore a pink sweater and white slacks and she smiled warmly when her eyes met Remo's eyes, which were so dark that they might be black. Remo was almost six feet tall and slim, with thick wrists that protruded from his rolled-up shirt sleeves.

"Where is she?" Remo said.

"Where's who?"

"C'mon, I don't have a lot of time. My crew's waiting outside and we've got to hurry to get this on the seven o'clock network news. Where is she?"

He drummed his fingers on the countertop.

"I'll take you to her," the girl said.

Remo shook his head.

"No. Just let me get this interview done and then I'll have some time to come back to talk to you."

"Promise?"

"Cross my heart and hope to die," Remo said.

"Room 27. End of the wing," the girl said, pointing toward a window.

"Anybody in the rooms around them?" Remo asked.

The girl threw Remo a nervous little glance. He explained quickly, "Nothing ruins an interview faster than somebody talking in the next room. You'll find that out when you're on television yourself."

The girl nodded. "No. Nobody on either side. They wanted it that way."

"Thanks. I'll be back."

Back at the car, Remo told Chiun, "I'll be a few minutes."

"Take your time. Just don't be untidy."

Remo heard voices inside Room 27 and went back to Room 26. The door was locked but he vibrated the knob quickly in his hand, back and forth, until the metal parts slipped and the knob turned easily. He locked the door quickly behind him.

Listening at the connecting doors between the rooms, Remo heard and recognized two of the voices.

There was Janie Baby, with her well-bred nasal whine that somehow changed into a smooth liquid soprano when she began to sing. There was the languid voice of her consort, the revolutionary lawyer-theoretician who lived with her in Malibu. Remo did not recognize any of the other voices.

Janie Baby: "Tony, run over the plan one more time so we all know what we're doing."

Tony: "I've gone over it three times already."

Janie Baby: "Then this time should be easy for you. Once more."

Cheer up, Remo thought. That's the price you have to pay for being the royal stud. It could have been worse. One of the other well-known protest leaders was wanted for selling drugs; another had married a Hollywood star and joined the middle class; another one was shilling for a guru.

Tony: "We bring the guns in under the boxes of food and hand them out. Janie, at 8:30, you call the press to a meeting at the rear of the crowd. That way, they won't be able to see anything. When you get started, we'll get the crowd to surge toward the gates. Our people will fire a couple of shots. The cops will fire back. By the time the press gets back there, it'll be a full-scale riot. Of course, we'll have witnesses who say the cops fired first. When the mob pushes through the gate, well have the explosives stashed next to the generator station in a box that looks like a reel of electric cable. We'll be long gone 'cause there's no point in taking a chance on getting hurt. Then after they put down the riot, probably during the night we'll trigger the explosives by radio and blow up the whole frigging plant."

Unknown voice: "People might get hurt."

Janie Baby: "You can't make an omelet without breaking some eggs."

Tony: "Right. That's not our problem. Anyway, tomorrow Janie'll hold a press conference and blame the shooting on the cops. We'll phony up some witnesses who saw them fire first."

Unknown voice: "What about the explosion?"

Janie Baby: "Leave that to me. It just proves what a shoddy unsafe operation this coal-burning monster is. Where's the radio transmitter to set off the charge?"

Tony: "It's under my mattress. Well leave it there until we want it so there's no accident."

Unknown voice: "I've put the guns at the bottom of the box of chicken salad sandwiches. It's marked on top."

Janie Baby: "Good. And the explosives?"

Voice: "Already in the trunk of the car."

Pause.

Janie Baby: "Okay. It's almost seven o'clock. We better get moving."

Remo waited while people shuffled around in the next room, then heard the front door open and close. He glanced out the edge of the drape at the front window and saw the singer, her husband and two other men walking toward a white Lincoln sedan, dripping with chrome and doodads. Presumably, Remo thought, their grass-fueled Volkswagen was at the florist for repairs.

There was no knob on Remo's side of the connecting doors, just a round smooth lock plate. Remo brought his right hand back to his hip and punched with his hard fingertips into the wood next to the round brass plate. The wood splintered as Remo's fingers drove into the core of the door. His fingertips nicked the lock mechanism, turned it and the door pushed open.

The single room looked like an illegal dump. Neither bed was made. A wastepaper basket was filled with beer cans and wine bottles and when it had overflowed, the room's occupants had made do by throwing cans and bottles anywhere. Butcher paper from sandwiches littered the floor. Half-eaten heroes were dropped on the dresser.

Remo peeked into the bathroom, curious to see how the well-bred who wanted to bring America to a new and brighter tomorrow of freedom and personal responsibility lived. The sink was pocked with beard stubble, but the free motel soap had not been opened. The bath towels had not been touched and the shower and tub were dry and unused. There were four beer cans on the vanity shelf next to the sink. There was a half-empty jar of no-fluorocarbon anti-perspirant next to the sink, along with a dozen cylindrical plastic bottles of multicolored pills.

"Better living through chemistry," Remo said aloud. He went back into the main room and flipped the mattress from one bed onto the floor. There was no radio transmitter under it.

Remo lifted up the second mattress and saw the transmitter, a square black box with dials, a chrome button and a pull-up antenna. Behind him, he heard the front door open.

"Well, well, well, what have we here?" a voice asked.

Remo looked over his shoulder and said, "Maid service. This room was due for a cleaning in 1946 and somehow we missed it."

The man standing in the doorway was a large blond with a slick brown tan. He wore white jeans. His biceps bulged from under his short-sleeved tan shirt and his lat muscles rippled as he folded his arms and looked at the radio transmitter on the bed.

"What's that?" he asked.

"A new organic mini-vacuum cleaner," Remo said. "It gets rid of all kinds of dirt. Want to see how it works?"

"No, wiseass. I just want to see you in the slammer for burglary."

He came into the room and closed the door behind him. Remo picked up the radio transmitter and let the mattress collapse back onto the bed. The blond man reached for the telephone on the end table near the door.

"Can't let you do that, friend," Remo said.

"Try and stop me," the burly blond said.

"Whatever makes you happy," Remo said.

He walked casually toward the blond who now had the phone in his hand. Remo reached out a finger and depressed the cutoff button.

The blond, with a nasty sneer on his face, tried to do two things at once. He slammed the receiver back down, hoping to smash it onto Remo's finger, and with the heel of his left hand he pushed at Remo's chest to try to shove him back into the room.

The receiver hit the phone base but missed Remo's finger. The blond felt his right hand being removed from the instrument by Remo's left hand. The heel of the big man's left hand slammed squarely against Remo's chest. To the blond, it felt like butting his hand against a brick wall. The shock wave raced back through his wrist, up his forearm and upper arm and made his shoulder shudder.

He swung wildly at Remo's head with his right hand. The punch missed.

"Isn't there any way you're going to behave yourself?" Remo asked.

"I'm gonna take your head off, sucker," the blond said.

Remo sighed. The blond threw another left hand and right hand at the slim man standing in front of him. Remo did not move, but somehow both punches missed. It was as if the smaller man had kept his feet rooted but had just swayed left and right out of the reach of the punches. The blond felt his long back muscles stretching painfully when the punches missed. He grabbed at the telephone and slapped it towards Remo's temple, but the instrument went over the top of Remo's head as he ducked. Then, as Remo came up, the blond felt himself lifted high into the air, and his 240 pounds were being thrown toward the back of the motel room. He wasn't spry enough or quick-witted enough to cushion his head before he butted skull first into the wall. The crunch of his head hitting the wall punched a foot-wide soft spot into the sheetrock of the wall, beneath the cheap metallic vinyl wallcovering. The blond groaned and fell into a lump.

Remo walked out the front door without looking back. If the man wasn't dead, that was all right. And if he was dead, that was all right too. What mattered was the big ugly Lincoln and making sure it did not get too far away.

He put the radio transmitter on the seat between himself and Chiun as he got into the rented car and drove quickly from the motel parking lot.

When he reached Clairburg four miles away, he saw the white Lincoln four cars ahead of him. With luck, he would get close on the open stretch of highway leading from the town to the electrical station.

They were just passing out of the town and moving back onto the main highway when Chiun said, "You are not going to tell me, are you?"

"Tell you what?"

"What is this black box?"

Remo watched ahead. The other cars had moved away from between his car and the white Lincoln. There was only three hundred yards now between the cars and Remo was steadily closing the gap.

"It's a toy," Remo said.

"How does it work?" Chiun asked. His long-fingernailed hands moved over to pick up the black box.

"I'll explain," Remo said. "First pull up the antenna."

Chiun's long fingers nipped at the round ball at the top of the retractable antenna and pulled it up to its full 15-inch height.

"What now?" he asked.

"There's a switch there that says on-off. Turn it to on," Remo said.

Without looking, he heard Chiun click the switch. He was only a hundred yards now behind the Lincoln. There were no other cars visible on the road.

"What next?" Chiun said. "Must I always drag everything out of you?"

"There is a battery/indicator light next to the on off switch," Remo said. "Tell me when it comes on."

"I like this," Chiun said. "I really like this."

"Just watch for the light," Remo said.

"It's on," Chiun said. "It's on. An orange light. It just came on."

Seventy-five yards.

"Now you see that button on top?" Remo asked.

"Yes."

"Do you know what'll happen if you press it?"

"What?" asked Chiun.

Fifty yards.

"Try it and find out."

"I want to know first," Chiun said. "What will happen if I press it?" But even as he spoke his index finger reached toward the chrome button.

"Watch that car up there," Remo said. Chiun looked up as he pressed the button.

There was a muffled thump in the Lincoln ahead of them and then a large explosion that lifted the car six feet up into the air. Sheets of white metal ripped from the car while it was airborne and flew even higher into the air. While the car was still off the ground, the gas tank exploded and turned the car into an oblong ball of flame, which hit back onto the roadway and careened forward until it slammed against a metal and concrete retaining wall.

It burned. There would be no gunfights tonight at the electrical station. No bombs planted. No semi-innocent people killed. Remo felt good about it.

Without slowing down, he skidded a U-turn in the highway, jumped the low concrete center divider and drove back toward the town.

"A boom," Chiun said.

"Bomb," said Remo. "And remember, no complaints about bombs ruining the perfection of an assassination. You did it yourself."

"You mean every time I press this button, a car will blow up?"

"No," said Remo.

"It has to be a white car?"

"No."

"An ugly white car?"

"No," said Remo. "It'll never work again."

Chiun rolled down his window and tossed the black transmitter far out into the weeds lining the road.

"Junk," he said. "What good is a piece of junk that only works once?"

"Just what I was thinking," Remo said.

There was a message for them when they returned to their motel room. Remo was to call his Aunt Lorraine right away. That meant Harold W. Smith, director of the secret agency CURE for which Remo worked as an assassin. This week it was Aunt Lorraine. Last week, it had been Uncle Howard and the week before that, Cousin Doreen. Remo wondered if the republic's secrets would really all go down the tube if the CURE director simply left a message for Remo to call Smith.

When the clerk told him that he should call Aunt Lorraine, Remo decided to test his theory.

"I don't have an Aunt Lorraine," he said.

"But that's what the message was," the clerk said. "Really. I took the call myself."

"Yes, but that's just a code," Remo said. "That's from a man named Smith who wants me to call him."

There was a pause. The clerk said, "Then why didn't he just say to call Mr. Smith?"

"Because he's afraid you'll tell the Russians. Worse yet, the Congress."

"Oh, I see," the clerk said. "Well, I have other things to do, sir, so I'd better get off this line."

"You're not calling the Russians, are you?" Remo asked.

"No, sir."

"All right. You'd better not because Smitty gets upset about things like that," Remo said.

The clerk gave him an open line and Remo dialed an 800 area code number which went through two switching devices before it finally rang inside a sanitarium in Rye, New York, where CURE's headquarters maintained its cover operation.

"Remo here," said Remo.

Smith's dry voice started out without any identification, but there was no mistaking the acid tones.

"Remo, do you know who Bobby Jack Billings is?"

Remo thought a moment before a picture of a fat face with a beer can implanted came into his mind.

"Yeah. He's the President's uncle or something."

"Brother-in-law," Smith said. "He's been kidnapped."

"Sounds good to me," Remo said as he hung up the telephone and disconnected it from the wall.

ABOUT THE AUTHORS

WARREN MURPHY was born in Jersey City, where he worked in journalism and politics until launching the *Destroyer* series with Richard Sapir in 1971. A screenwriter (*Lethal Weapon II, The Eiger Sanction*) as well as a novelist, Murphy's work has won a dozen national awards, including multiple Edgars and Shamuses. He has lectured at many colleges and universities, and is currently offering writing lessons at his website, warrenmurphy.com. A Korean War veteran, some of Murphy's hobbies include golf, mathematics, opera, and investing. He has served on the board of the Mystery Writers of America, and has been a member of the Screenwriters Guild, the Private Eye Writers of America, the International Association of Crime Writers, and the American Crime Writers League. He has five children: Deirdre, Megan, Brian, Ardath, and Devin.

RICHARD BEN SAPIR was a New York native who worked as an editor and in public relations before creating *The Destroyer* series with Warren Murphy. Before his untimely death in 1987, Sapir had also penned a number of thriller and historical mainstream novels, best known of which were *The Far Arena, Quest,* and *The Body,* the last of which was made into a film. The book review section of the New York Times called him "a brilliant professional."

Made in the USA
Columbia, SC
27 October 2023

25030806R00080